WE'RE ON OUR WAY TO ITALY!

Haydn Middleton

SCHOLASTIC

Scholastic Children's Books,
Commonwealth House, 1-19 New Oxford Street,
London, WC1A 1NU, UK
a division of Scholastic Ltd
London ~ New York ~ Toronto ~ Sydney ~ Auckland
Mexico City ~ New Delhi ~ Hong Kong

Published in the UK by Scholastic Ltd, 2000

ISBN 0 439 99621 X

Typeset by TW Typesetting, Midsomer Norton, Somerset
Printed by The Bath Press, Bath

2 4 6 8 10 9 7 5 3 1

1

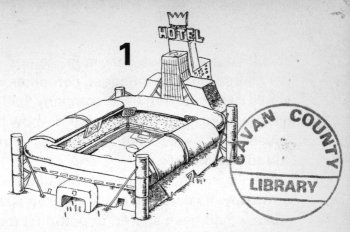

"My lords, ladies and gentlemen!" boomed the announcer over the top-volume PA system. "Players, supporters and officials of today's visitors, Hull City: welcome, welcome, welcome to the official opening of the Majestic Stadium – the brand new home of Castle Albion FC!"

In the warm May sunshine, an enormous cheer went up from 25,000 fans. It was a wonder they had any voices left at all. For the past two hours they had whooped, yelled, roared and hollered at one pre-match spectacle after another. Skydivers, marching bands, fireworks, songs from All Saints, a thousand-woman dancing troupe, a weepy speech from guest-of-honour Kevin Keegan.

There had never been such a build-up to a Nationwide League Division Three relegation clash. But this was no ordinary Saturday after-noon football match. For today, after almost a whole season of building delays, the stadium was hosting its first fixture. At last, the dream of

Castle Albion player-chairman James Prince had come true. The teenaged computer whizz – whose Majestic Software company had made him megabucks all over the world – now had his very own Majestic Stadium for his hometown club to play in.

And what a stadium it was! Standing near the motorway inside acres of car-parking space, no expense had been spared in putting it together. Twenty-five thousand blue and white seats, a retractable roof for when it rained, a state-of-the-art undersoil heating system, hospitality boxes, banqueting suites, a shopping "village" behind one goal, a towering luxury hotel behind the other.

This, truly, was a football ground fit for the twenty-first century. Which was all rather weird for most people connected with the Albion. Because their last ground – Ash Acre – had never quite made it into the twentieth. But a tiny bit of that dear old town-centre ruin had been brought to the Majestic today. Or, to be precise, three tiny bits. All wrapped up in three plastic bags that were being held by a man and two boys at the entrance to the players' tunnel.

"And now," cried the announcer, "just before the teams take to the pitch to continue this historic day's entertainment, Castle Albion Supporters Club Chairman Mr Rocky Mitford will perform a short ceremony. In this he will be assisted by two young players who need no introduction from me: Albion's schoolboy superstars Luke Green and 'Cool' Frederick Dulac!"

A roar even louder than before greeted the three as they stepped out on to the lush turf. Rocky Mitford, a big curly-haired guy in a 1970s Albion replica shirt, strode straight for the centre-circle. The two lads broke into a trot towards each goal – Cool Fred in his wraparound shades, Luke in his trademark trainers.

This grass felt *so* springy under Luke's soles. He had played in a Cup Final at Wembley, but this felt twice as bouncy as that. And although the Majestic wasn't as big as Wembley, it *seemed* even bigger – maybe because all the fans were so far away from the pitch. (At Ash Acre, you could just about chat with the fans from the centre-spot. Here you would need a mobile phone.)

"Rocky, Luke and Fred have brought a little bit of history with them to the Majestic Stadium today," the announcer explained as the two boys reached the goalmouths, and – like Rocky in the centre circle – began to undo their plastic bags. "They've brought some grass-cuttings from the pitch back at Ash Acre. Hey guys, I'm surprised you could find that much grass *on* the pitch there! I thought it was all dried mud! Now they're going to sprinkle it on the pitch here. It's their way of linking up the past to the present. And you know, they're right: we must never forget where we came from..." He paused for effect before delivering his punchline, "... just in case anyone ever suggests we should go back there again!"

Luke frowned as he took his handful of clippings and scattered it over the goal line. The Majestic was mighty impressive, but there was no need to knock Ash Acre. He still loved the old place. He'd had some of the best times of his life there. So had Albion – not least in beating Villa, Newcastle and Liverpool on their miraculous FA Cup-winning campaign of the season before.

"Let's hear it for Rocky, Luke and Frederick!" the announcer whipped up the crowd. "And what a good job they just brought some historic *grass* – and not those historic old Ash Acre toilets!"

Back at Albion's old home, the PA system usually packed up after a couple of minutes. Luke half-wished that would happen here, just to shut this bloke up.

But there was no chance of that. As Rocky walked back to the touchline, and Luke and Fred trotted over to the centre-circle, the rest of the Albion team appeared one by one. Each got a booming namecheck from Mr Microphone: "Put your hands together please for ... goalie

'Madman' Mort ... full-backs Dennis Meldrum and Craig Edwards ... centre-half and skipper Stuart 'Gaffer' Mann ... midfield maestros Chrissie Pick, Trinidad's own Narris Phiz and Michael 'Half-Fat' Milkes ... and finally our trusty twin strike-force: homegrown Carl Davey, and that matchless goal-machine from Armenia – the one and only Dogan 'The Dog' Mezir!"

The players formed a circle, then turned with a big wave for the mad-keen Albion faithful (and the hooting, jeering travellers from Hull). The announcer then introduced the subs on the touchline, but saved his biggest shout for, "The young man who has made all this possible. He's a winner, he's a star, he makes dreams come true: our player-chairman, Mr James 'Jimbo' Prince!"

And out of the tunnel came a skinny little guy in glasses and a tracksuit. His corkscrew hair flew all over the place as he ran for the centre-spot, with both arms up to salute the crowd's applause.

Luke, still clutching his plastic bag (with a few blades of grass in it for himself), closed his eyes. *Don't fall over*, he prayed, *please don't fall over*... For Jimbo didn't often run for more than twenty yards without taking a tumble. Computerwise, this boy was Champions League. Footballwise, he wasn't even toddler-group standard. But because he now owned the club, he'd made sure he was picked to play in quite a few games. For the past two weeks, however, he'd been unavailable for selection, thanks to "an iffy toe".

He didn't fall over. He got to the centre-spot, clenched his fists and milked the crowd's polite hand-claps for all he was worth. But Luke couldn't help thinking of one guy who *hadn't* been name-checked. The guy who really *was* Castle Albion. If you cut this man, his blood ran (pretty slowly) in blue and white hoops. There he was over on the touchline now, one hand deep in the pocket of his sheepskin coat, the other tugging nervily at his bushy white beard: Benny Webb, club manager.

Luke loved this guy to bits. So did everyone else in the Albion squad. He was utterly unique in football management. He didn't really have a clue about tactics. At times he didn't even seem clear about the laws of the game. His favourite form of discipline was a clip round the ear (not just for players but also for reporters who annoyed him). But inside him the true spirit of football burned *so* brightly. If you stood next to him for a minute you could feel the glow. Somehow or other, Benny understood football. He knew what made it tick. It was the same thing that made *him* tick. And on a good day he could pass that thing on to Luke and Fred and all the other lads.

But since an unforgettable night in Paris two weeks before, Jimbo hadn't said a word to Big Ben. And he certainly wasn't going to have the name "Webb" boomed out in *his* new stadium today. Some day soon, the two main men at Albion would have to go head to head and sort out their differences once and for all. Not now, though.

Now, after all the fireworks, skydivers and dancers, it was time to kick leather.

2

The black-and-amber-clad Hull side charged out of the tunnel with one aim in mind – to poop this party. They didn't care if they played Albion at Ash Acre, the Majestic Stadium or on the forecourt of a drive-through McDonald's. All that mattered to them was a point. One point. The sort you got for a draw. Because that's all they needed to make themselves safe for another season.

At kick-off time Hull lay 22nd out of the 24 teams in the Third Division. Albion lay 23rd, with three points less and by far the worst goal difference in the League. Propping up the lot lay poor old Chester City, just one point behind Albion. "So remind me," said striker Carl Davey to Luke as Gaffer tossed up for ends, "if we win today we're safe – right?"

"Right," nodded Luke. He was half Carl's age but twice as clued-up. "As long as Chester don't win as well. Then nothing would be decided till the last game of the season, next week."

Carl looked more worried than ever. "But what if we draw and Chester win? Does that mean *we'd* get relegated to the Football Conference?"

"I think we'd better leave the sums till later," suggested Luke, nodding at Jimbo who – with special permission – was about to take the opening-day kick-off before leaving the pitch. "You crack a hatful, Carl, and we'll be all right!"

But that afternoon, cracking a hatful was easier said than done. It was just so strange to be playing at home – yet not at Ash Acre. Every time Luke paused for a breather, there was no nostril-clogging stink of ancient, burnt onions and ghastly-burgers. The ball seemed to get caught up in the long grass, rather than bouncing all over the place like at Ash Acre. And although the distant crowd was twice as big as there, they seemed to be making only half as much noise.

Not that Rocky Mitford and the Supporters' Chorus had much to make a noise about. For the first twenty-five minutes Albion barely strung two passes together. Almost everyone in a hooped shirt looked sluggish and out of sorts. Luke in right midfield, along with Frederick at sweeper, played their usual smart games. But two schoolboys can't carry a whole professional team. Time after time, their golden through-balls and crosses were turned to lead by the players who got on the end of them. And

Hull, who had started off pretty poorly themselves, began to realize that this game was
there to be won.

So they did what you have to do if you want
to win a football match. They scored a goal. The
first-ever goal at the Majestic Stadium. And it
went straight through goalie Madman Mort's
legs. It wasn't even a proper shot. Just a toe-
poke from the Hull number ten as he darted
forward to cut out a disastrous pass from
Dennis to Craig across the six-yard box.
Suddenly there was real noise – all of it coming
from the seats behind the Hull goal:

**"Best Ground in the Con-frence! You've got the
Best Ground in the Con-frence!"**

Rocky then tried to get some Albion chants
going, but it was an uphill struggle. Maybe if
that retractable roof had been on, it would have
helped. Luke could see Benny going ape by the
dug-out – but nothing he screamed was
carrying across the pitch either. And, in spite of
what everyone was expecting, he didn't take
the chance to scream it all again at half-time.

Instead, when the players trooped into the
dressing-room, he was busy scribbling away on
a sheet of paper. "Right," he said when he'd
finished. He held up the sheet. "This," he
explained in a weird, flat, quiet voice, "is my
letter of resignation."

"What?!" shrieked everyone. Benny loved to

spring surprises. They kept people on their toes, he said. But this was more like a shock. The deadly serious kind of shock that can get a whole squad of footballers rushed to hospital.

He silenced them with one raised hand. "Diabolical," he solemnly went on. "That's the only word for your performance out there. Plainly I am not getting my message as a manager across to you. In that sense, I'm not doing my job properly. So maybe it's time for me to move on. I won't say any more now. You know how I like the game played. You know what habits I like my players to have. If we lose this game, then that's it for me: I'll be off."

He folded the sheet, slipped it carefully into a sheepskin pocket, sat down in the corner, then silently reached for his tea.

No one said a word. The squad just stared at him – aghast. *Resign?!* Luke could see all the others were sweating just like him. There was no way of imagining Castle Albion without Benny Webb. You couldn't even begin to picture it. But he was such an off-the-wall sort of guy, he *might* just go. Oh wow…

For once, Jimbo wasn't around to give his own usual half-time pep-talk. (He was too busy touring the hospitality bars and popping champagne corks with his billionaire business guests.) So apart from the odd tea-slurp, the silence deepened. Then suddenly Benny looked up. "Oh, you two," he said to Luke and Fred, "you've done fine. Go out and enjoy the half-time entertainment."

The boys looked at the others, got the nod, and scooted off. To be honest, it was a relief to get out of there. But there was a special reason why Luke wanted to see the old hippie guitar-player who was belting out his latest single over the Majestic's wide open spaces. He happened to be Luke's dad; TAFKAG (The Artist Formerly Known As Green) to everyone else.

After a lifetime of musical obscurity, he had shot to fame by recording Albion's Cup Final single the year before. *Castle Rap* – featuring a killer spoken-word section by Cool F himself – had gone gold or platinum all over the world. Now his first album had just been released. And it too was rocketing up the charts, everywhere from Afghanistan to Zambia.

No one was quite sure *why*. Half the people who bought TAFKAG's stuff thought it was meant to be funny. The rest found something deep and meaningful in lyrics like "*Clouds in the mirror, Dust on the lake, The newt in the ceiling won't give me a break*". That's what he was singing right now – and giving it absolutely *loads*. Luke and Fred exchanged glances, raised an eyebrow each, then nodded along to the rest of it. But their minds were still on Benny.

Then it was back to business. Albion had to

grab a goal back. But in spite of Benny's awful threat, they were almost as underwhelming now as they had been before the break. Luke curled in cross after cross from the right touchline. Yet Carl looked as if he could *walk* to Hull and back before he ever stuck the ball in the net. And as for his strike-partner Dogan Mezir – the one-time sheep-farmer from Armenia, and Albion's record signing – he seemed to keep running in completely the wrong direction. If this had been a sheepdog trial and not a footie match, shaggy old SuperDog would have been disqualified yonks ago.

The minutes ticked away. Apart from at the Hull end, the stadium got more and more eerily quiet. In a last desperate throw, Benny subbed Carl, Dog and Chrissie Pick with youngsters Casper Franks, Keats Aberdeen and Darius Aldershot. They ran about a lot more, but not a lot more usefully.

Luke looked up at the enormous video screen. The clock showed three minutes left. What a way to christen the new stadium! So much for Fortress Majestic. This really hadn't been in the script at all. And nor had Benny Webb resigning after the very first game here. But he couldn't go, could he? He *couldn't*! It made Luke's knees shake just to think about it. Oh no, *no*!

Albion ploughed forward for yet another

soggy blitz on the Hull goal. Narris laid a reasonable pass into Half-Fat's path. He looked up, saw Darius making a good run towards the far post, and lofted the ball up to him.

Now you know the phrase "a rubbish cross"? What Half-Fat had just delivered was a rubbish cross. So rubbish, it could have had fish bones and potato peel stuck to it. Not high enough, not far enough, nowhere near accurate enough. A huge sigh went up from the three Albion sides of the ground. Giggles broke out at the Hull end. Even one or two of the Hull players had a quick smile.

Then it happened. The game's one moment of class. A moment worthy of this sparkling stadium on its opening day. It was as if, up to this point, everything had been going on in slow motion. But as Half-Fat's pathetic cross began to drop down, somebody suddenly got the speed right. Cool Frederick Dulac.

Luke almost *heard* him accelerate up from the back before he saw him. A blur of blue-and-white, zooming in on the falling ball, smacking it on the volley from thirty yards, leaving the Hull keeper for dead. And even before it hit the net, Fred was looking down and adjusting the hang of his combat-style shorts. They didn't call this boy cool for nothing!

The home faithful danced and leapt and hugged one another. Albion 1, Hull 1! Frederick had saved the home team's bacon. They couldn't snatch a winner in the short time left, but at least they had a point. Albion hadn't lost. Fortress Majestic hadn't fallen under its first bombardment. And that meant that Benny could tear up his bit of paper and stay on in the job that God had made for him.

But afterwards the news from elsewhere wasn't so good. Chester had drawn too. So Albion still needed a result from their last game – away at Northampton – if they were definitely going to survive. And that wouldn't be easy.

3

On Tuesday morning Luke and Fred didn't go to school. Instead, one of Jimbo's chauffeurs took them straight to the Majestic for a training session with the rest of the squad. The boys' headmistress didn't mind them training once a week. As an Albion season-ticket holder herself, she knew the club would sink without the two of them. But when they arrived in the vast players' and officials' car park, a mass fight seemed to be taking place in one of the corners.

"No, no, no, no, NO, NO, NO!" they heard as they got out of their limo and passed by on their way to the stadium entrance. It wasn't a fight – just Benny Webb being ambushed by the media on his way in.

"There is no question whatsoever of me answering any questions about Rome. Not at this crucial stage of the Nationwide League Division Three season. *All* my thoughts and plans at this point in time are geared towards getting a result at Northampton on Saturday. *Only* when we've secured our League status for another season will I even *think* about Rome. And I'd be grateful if you'd not mention it to any of my lads either. They've got enough on their plates as it is."

Luke looked at Fred and rolled his eyes. Rome... For the past two weeks, Benny had made that a taboo word in the dressing-room. "First things first," he kept warning them. All the talk had to be about the League, not the Cup. The UEFA Cup, that was. The final of which was coming up in a fortnight's time, in Rome's 80,000-capacity Olympic Stadium.

Two teams had battled their way through all the gruelling rounds. One of them was the Spanish superclub, Barcelona. The other was – and it's probably best to take a long, deep breath before reading this: Castle Albion!!!

Yes, *this* Castle Albion. Benny Webb's Albion. Luke and Fred's Albion. The club currently lying 23rd in Division Three. If ever a club had a split personality, it was Albion. The year before, they had finished 23rd as well – but also managed to win the FA Cup. This year they had played like pants against the likes of Peterborough, Barnet and Lincoln, while disposing of Bayern Munich, Spartak Moscow and Paris St Germain *en route* to the UEFA Cup final. If Benny had said it once, he'd said it a million times: on their day, Albion could beat *anyone*. Sadly, they could be stuffed solid by anyone too.

"But Mr Webb, Mr Webb!!" one reporter was yelling above the rest as Benny tried to fight his way through to Luke and Fred. "Can you tell us if you've patched up your relationship with Mr Prince yet? Are you on speaking terms?"

Benny's face flushed a deep purple. "I'm not prepared to talk about that either," he muttered, struggling on. "Mr Prince and I are both one hundred per cent behind each other in wanting the best for Castle Albion FC. That's all you need to know."

"But Benny!" shouted another reporter, a woman this time. "This morning Mr Prince declared himself fit and available to play in both the Northampton game *and* the Barcelona match."

"Oh, did he?" asked Benny, pausing. This was obviously news to him. Luke swallowed hard too. Things were already tricky enough, without Jimbo making a comeback. With some players, their name on the teamsheet is worth a two-goal start. With Jimbo, it was like finding yourself ten-nil down.

"How does that fit in with your selection plans, Benny?" asked the silvery-haired man from *The Times*. "Word is that you dropped Mr Prince for the UEFA Cup semi-final in Paris, and that the two of you haven't spoken since."

"No comment," grunted Benny, at last breaking free of all the scribblers and snappers, putting his arms round the shoulders of Luke and Fred, and guiding them on through the towering entrance. Once they were inside, he let out a great sigh and seemed to sag where he stood on the lush, deep-pile carpet, with the new CAFC logo printed all over it.

"Sorry to be leaning on you lads," Benny murmured (and he *was* quite heavy). "That just took the wind out of my sails a bit. After Paris, I'd thought Jimbo had realized how useless he was. I never thought he'd ever try to get back in the team. It's really hit me for six, this has..."

Luke, bracing his back to take the strain, knew what the Boss meant. Jimbo had been so awful in the games before the Paris semi-final, that with only minutes to the kick-off Benny had suddenly snapped. As the rest of the team looked on, gobsmacked, he dropped the player-chairman on the spot. That was the act of a very brave man. The player-chairman could throw a twenty-minute tantrum if someone put half-a-spoonful too much sugar in his half-time tea. But now, to be dropped from the team that he actually, lock-stock-and-barrel, *owned*...

At first Jimbo had thought it was a joke. When the truth at last hit home, he just stalked out of the dressing-room, then jetted right out of France. From then until the day of the Hull game, he had been all over the globe on business. But only the players knew that he'd been axed in Paris. And all of them, like Benny, had thought his injured pride would make him retire. Surely he would now hang up his boots (although he would probably miss the peg). The *last* thing they expected was for Princey to announce his comeback!

Just as Benny's weight was starting to make Luke and Fred buckle too, a guy in a blue track-suit bounced into view from the weights room. It was Terry Vaudeville, the club's long-serving physio and Benny's right-hand man. "Oh wow, he's heard the news, has he?" he asked the boys with a nod at the Boss.

" 'Fraid so," puffed Luke, almost keeling over now.

"Allow me to take this weight off your shoulders," grinned Terry, yanking Benny upright and straightening his sheepskin coat. "Thanks for your support!"

"We'll – er – go and get changed then?" said Luke.

"You do that," said Terry. "The Boss and me had better start sorting out the team for Saturday. Find a spot for our dear chairman." He hushed his voice and winked. "I know where we'd have put him in my day: right back off the field! Or was it left back in the dressing-room? What a turn-up for the books, eh? Young Princey really knows how to put the cat among the pigeons, don't he!"

4

The training-session went quite well – mainly because Jimbo didn't come anywhere near it. He knew how risky these things could be. Too many times he'd picked up a niggling injury just before an important game. It was almost as if his team-mates were *trying* to nobble him and put him out of action!

But he spent the rest of that day doing media interviews. He explained his absence since Paris as purely due to "business commitments and an iffy toe", and assured everyone that he was "raring to go" in both Northampton and Rome. BRING ON RIVALDO! was one of the evening newspaper headlines. *Prince vows to drive Barcelona's star from Brazil nuts!* said another.

He also announced that he'd arranged an "exhibition" match against an FA Premiership XI as a warm-up for the UEFA Cup Final. "The Majestic Stadium deserves to be graced by top-flight players," he said. "Our fans deserve to see more than Third Division cloggers and hackers week in, week out." Luke could just imagine the look on Benny's face when he read that. (Not to mention the faces of all the outraged cloggers and hackers of Division Three.)

But the next morning, the papers' back pages were full of another Jimbo-related story. This time, no one was claiming that JP himself was behind it, but apparently the world of football had been rocked by a new rumour.

"It's madness!" shrieked Luke's mum, screwing up her *Daily Mail* in disgust as Luke came down for breakfast. "Sheer and utter *madness*!"

"There, there, dear," said Luke's stepdad Rodney, wiping his hands on his pinny, then starting to make some toast for Luke. "It's only a rumour. Some bored journalist probably just made it up." But Luke could see that behind his glasses, Rod looked anxious too.

"What is it?" Luke asked, reaching for the newspaper. "What's happened?"

"Well – nothing," Rodney told him. "Nothing for sure, yet..."

"How could he even *think* of it!" Luke's mum raved on. "After everything Benny Webb's done for Castle Albion! He's pulled us up by the boot-laces and put us slap-bang in the centre of the world football map! Now *this*!"

Rod and Luke blinked at each other. It still amazed them to hear her talk with such passion about the Beautiful Game. She had once hated it so much, even the sight of a cheese football had made her blood start to boil. She had strictly forbidden Luke ever to watch a match, let alone play in one. So for over a year he'd had to keep his Albion career a complete secret from her.

And that wasn't easy, because pretty well everyone else in Britain knew all about it. But with a lot of help from his dad, his stepdad, his Nan and Grandpa and his headmistress, Luke had managed it. And then came Paris. Her conversion.

It had happened in the celebrations after Albion's fab semi-final victory. That was when she found that her son had been playing behind her back. Then suddenly, miraculously, she saw the light. Or rather, she was *shown* the light. By spending several hours in the company of the smoochiest presenter in television history – ITV's Mr Football, Des Lynam. No one knew exactly what Des said to win Luke's mum over as he whisked her off towards the Arc de Triomphe. But whatever it was, when he returned her to her hotel she was a changed woman. And she'd stayed that way ever since.

Finally Luke smoothed out the *Mail*'s back page enough to read the bad news:

WEBB OUT, VENNERS IN!!
PRINCE TO BRING IN VENABLES IN TIME FOR
UEFA FINAL!

Luke felt a cold shiver run the length of his spine. He had nothing against Terry Venables. Quite the opposite. He'd been a great England manager, and Luke thought he should never have lost that job. But to give him *Benny*'s job... Just days before the biggest match in Albion's history...

"It's an absolute disgrace," Luke's mum went on, adjusting her Albion bobble hat but not noticing the end of her Albion scarf dangling in her unfinished bowl of Sugar Puffs. "Terry Fennerballs! Or whatever his stupid name is! What's *he* ever done? He didn't do a *thing* when he managed Arsenal!"

"Er – Tottenham, dear," Rodney dared to correct her, but she didn't hear.

"And Benny Webb might be a sad and hopeless human being! And why he wears that *beard*, I'll never know! But as a *manager*... Look at what he's done over the past two seasons! First of all winning the Worthington Cup..."

"Um – that's the *FA* Cup, dear," Rodney tried in vain to remind her.

"Then getting us to the final of the Champions' League..."

There was no point in Rod or Luke telling her it was actually the UEFA Cup. When she got this wound-up – which she did pretty often – she wouldn't listen if the Queen, Pope and Prime Minister joined forces to try to put her straight.

"Am I the only person who can see what a recipe for disaster this is!" she cried, picking up her Albion klaxon horn and giving it a monster blast.

"Hey, listen," cried Rodney, turning up the kitchen radio. "It's Jimbo."

"*I have only this to say*," came the familiar sound of JP's ratty, squeaky voice. "*Any stories linking Castle Albion FC with Mr Terry Venables at this point are totally out of order. All that matters to the club right now is getting the right result at Northampton on Saturday, with Mr Webb in charge of team affairs.*"

"Right," said Rodney slowly. "But what about *after* the Northampton game?"

Luke puffed out his bean-filled cheeks. "I guess we'll soon find out."

"*Arrrrrgggggggghhhhhhhhh!*" went Luke's mum, quivering so much with fury now that she couldn't get a single note out of her horn. "If you were half a man, Rodney, you'd go straight up to that Majestic Stadium and *kick* little Mr Moneybags right through his own retractable roof!! That would teach him!!!"

5

"Phew," said Terry Vaudeville as the team coach nosed its way through the crowds outside Northampton Town's still-quite-new Sixfields Stadium. "What a load of Cobblers!"

"Steady on, Tel," said shaven-headed Chrissie Pick. "It doesn't look as good as the Majestic, I grant you. But I've seen a lot worse."

"Nah, nah," smiled the chirpy physio, "that's what Northampton are called. 'The Cobblers.' That's their nickname. They used to make shoes here, I think."

"They used to be some team, too," Gaffer nodded. "Back in the Sixties, they went from the bottom Division to the top in just five seasons." He nodded harder, looking grimmer. "All under the same manager too."

Ruel Bibbo, who ran the club's Centre of Excellence, gripped his arm. "C'mon Gaffer," he said. "Ben's in charge here and he's gonna stay in charge."

"At least till after this game," murmured Half-

Fat. "And then what? Terry flippin' Venables?!"

"Hey, that's enough of that!" laughed Terry. "There's only room for one Terry V at this club!"

"Right," agreed Madman. "So Princey'll probably sack you too."

"Lads, lads," cried Benny from his seat beside the driver. "I don't wanna hear another word about managers – past, present or future – till we've done the business here today. Look at those loyal Albion fans out there. They've come here in their thousands, and all they want to see is Albion safe for another season in the League. Everything else is just icing on the jelly."

Dennis Meldrum frowned. "Don't you mean on the cake, Boss?"

"You haven't seen Carl's legs," smiled Darius, who was sitting next to the wavy-haired striker. "They're wobblin' all over the place here!"

"I'll soon put that right," said Craig Edwards, producing a big juicy pineapple from his kit-bag. "All he needs is a nice firm hit from this. Right, Carl?"

"Right," agreed Carl, giving him a thumbs-up. It was a vital part of his pre-match preparation. If Craig didn't belt him on the bottom with a fresh pineapple, he honestly believed he had no chance of hitting the net. But once they were all inside the dressing-room – and Carl had gratefully taken his whack – the spirits of the squad seemed to sink. Luke understood why. You only had to look at the teamsheet. There at number ten, in place of Narris, was quite possibly the worst player on two legs in all Europe: James Prince.

"He wrote his own name on," Benny explained after a brief, passionate team-talk. "Told me there was no question of him being left out. Otherwise he would have called off the game. And that would've meant automatic relegation."

"The little nerd!" growled Narris. "Where is he, anyway?"

Benny shrugged. "He travelled here in his own helicopter, and he's asked for a separate dressing-room."

"Why?" asked Keats. "Does he think we smell or something?"

"No, he's worried about that injury jinx of his," Benny said. "He didn't want to risk getting too close to any of you lot before the kick-off."

"Shame," sighed Craig, fondling the now badly bruised pineapple. "I know just where this could have accidentally ended up."

"OK, OK," called Benny, clapping his hands. "No good's gonna come from that sort of talk. You've already got a mountain to climb here today. Northampton need three points to be sure of getting into the play-offs. Just give it your best shot – and go for the win we so desperately need ourselves."

"Or at least hope Chester don't beat York at home," added Dennis.

"Don't you worry about that! Now get out there and fight for your League lives!" Luke heard a sudden crack in the Boss's voice. As everyone got up and headed for the tunnel, Luke looked back and saw all the emotion in the big guy's face – well, in the parts of it not covered by beard and moustache.

Every ball that was kicked or headed or caught today would be kicked, headed and caught by the Bossman too. Luke knew then that, whatever he might say, Benny Webb would *never* resign from this job. For him, it wasn't a job at all, it was a love affair. He was Albion Till He Died. And then in the afterlife as well.

Inevitably, in the tunnel, Carl edged up to Luke with a puzzled look on his face. "We've got to *win*, right?" he whispered. "To have any chance of staying up?"

"Well, we've got one more point than Chester," Luke answered, "but they've got a miles better goal-difference. Really, we've got to do better than them."

Carl's face darkened. "So we're not really playing Northampton, but Chester?"

"Well, in a way."

"And there's no question at all of away goals counting double?"

29

"No, Carl. This isn't a European match. We're in Northampton."

"I knew that!" Carl answered sharply, almost proudly. "I definitely knew that!"

6

Jimbo appeared on the pitch only as Gaffer was tossing up with the Cobblers' skipper. An odd mix of sounds greeted him from around the ground.

On the claret-and-white sides crammed with Northampton fans, there were huge cheers. (Jimbo was always the most popular Albion player with other teams' fans. To be fair, he was always a lot more use to the opposition than he was to Albion.) But from the jampacked visitors' section, there came only a ripple of applause (from Albionites who never forgot that he had once saved their cash-strapped club from going out of business), a few hisses from Benny's hardcore supporters, and a mass *whoosh!* of eyebrows being raised.

Princey probably heard none of it. All his attention was on the small, middle-aged woman who trotted out beside him as far as the touchline. This was Mrs Doris Plunkett, his own personal faith healer and quite possibly his best

31

friend. Her main job was to get JP on to the "correct spiritual plane" to do his best over ninety minutes. To that end, she had now made him mumble, over and over, his "mantra" for the day. Luke caught an earful as he got into position himself. And although the situation here was so serious, he couldn't help smiling.

Through gritted teeth Jimbo was saying, as if his life depended on it: "...*Darren Anderton ... I am at least as good a footballer as Darren Anderton...*"

Just you believe it, thought Luke. It did, after all, offer some hope to the rest of the team. For if Jimbo played anything like the real Darren Anderton, then he would surely go off injured way before the end of the game.

But it didn't turn out like that. The next ninety minutes were among the most uncomfortable Luke had ever spent. It must have been even worse for the fans – from both sides. There was so much at stake that neither team seemed able to cope with the pressure. Every time a player managed to control the ball, he had a sudden attack of the jitters, and promptly gave it away again.

But very few got as far as controlling it in the first place. Slices, miskicks, airshots – you could have compiled a whole video with the title *Awful Albion and Not-A-Lot-of-Bottle Northampton*. Even Luke looked off-song. Though in his case, he did have an excuse. Playing closest to Jimbo in midfield, he was responsible for keeping the ball *away* from the player-chairman as much as possible. That often meant going for balls he had no real chance of winning. But at least he made sure JP didn't get a single touch before the interval.

Over in the dug-out, Benny stayed pretty quiet. In fact for minutes on end he looked like a dead sheep on the bench in his massive coat. He wasn't a lot more talkative in the dressing-room at half-time. There were no two ways about it. All the tension over his future was getting to him. It was getting to the players as well. "How can we express ourselves when all these question marks are hanging over us like daggers?" moaned Dennis, who co-wrote novels with Craig in his spare time.

"He's right," said Chrissie. "It's putting us off our stroke. We can't play our natural game. Every time I look up and see Princey, I think of Terry Venables."

"Must be confusing," admitted Ruel. "Where is Jimbo, anyway?"

"Getting another mantra off Mrs Plunkett," spat Narris. "I'd suggest: '*I am well past my sell-by date and should be put down immediately by a qualified vet.*' "

"Lads, lads," breathed Benny, hunched up sheepily in the corner. "This won't win us any points, will it? We've just got to keep plugging away. It'll come."

The trouble was, Benny didn't say exactly *what* would come. And what did come, in the sixty-eighth minute, was ... trouble. In a great Jimbo-sized dollop.

Up till then, Princey hadn't gone anywhere near his own penalty area. Luke made sure of that. Whenever he started drifting back, the Studless Sensation would wave him upfield again – or, at a pinch, actually tug him away. ("We need you where it counts," he'd explain. "Where you can do most damage to *them*.") But when Gaffer conceded a corner, no one spotted Jimbo suddenly gallop back as far as the six-yard box. Or not till it was too late.

The Cobblers' clever corner-kicker spotted him though. Ignoring his own team-mates' signals to try a move that they had practised in training, he drove the ball low and hard straight at the player-chairman. Luke made a lunge to get to the ball first. But it whistled past him – and smacked Jimbo in the stomach.

Now most pro footballers would never let that happen. And if they did, they would *never* do what Jimbo did next. Sheer instinct would stop them. Common sense would stop them. But Jimbo had neither. So, as he toppled backwards, he clapped both hands round the ball and *caught* it!

No Albion player appealed as the ref blew up and pointed to the spot. Even the whole Man U team plus Sir Alex Ferguson couldn't have disputed this decision. It was a penalty with a capital P. P for Prince. P for Prat-of-the-Season. P for Perfect-Way-To-Make-Sure-Albion-Lose-And-Get-Relegated. Right?

Well, not quite. It's never over till the Fat Lady Sings. And when it came to penalties against Albion, it was never over till the Fat Laddy Springs. The fat lad in question being keeper Madman Mort – never less than half-a-dozen pies overweight, but one of the best penalty-savers in the modern game. He had the statistics to prove it. Eighteen pens faced in the past three seasons, none conceded. He didn't even practise saving them. It was just a weird knack he had.

Even so, Luke could never bear to watch. As the home fans' roars of delight died down, and the Albion Massive began their boos and catcalls to put off the taker, he turned his back on the goal, shut his eyes, then prayed hard.

And that day, as usual with spot-kicks, God must have been wearing blue-and-white hoops. From the sudden silence on three sides of the ground, Luke knew Madman must have pulled it off yet again. He swivelled round, then joined all but one of the other Albion outfield players in diving on top of the Supersaver.

The one who didn't was Jimbo, still rubbing his tum. But when Terry shot to his feet and signalled that he might want to come off, he firmly shook his head.

As the game re-started, the celebrations of Rocky Mitford and Co briefly seemed to get much louder. Then, ten minutes later, although nothing remotely worth cheering had happened on the pitch, another great shout went up. Four minutes after that, it happened for a third time.

Several Albion players swapped puzzled looks. It was as if the visiting faithful had started watching another game. (And no one could have blamed them for that. The entertainment rating here at the Sixfields was hardly five-star.) Then Luke twigged. They weren't watching another game. They were *listening* to it. On radio earphones: Chester v York. And from what he'd heard, York must now be well ahead. A fact that, moments later, Rocky and Co confirmed:

"Three-nil to York Ci-ty!
Three-nil to York Ci-ty!
La-la La Laaaa! La-la La Laaaaaa!"

Luke saw Carl scratch his head at that. It was anyone's guess what he thought this meant for Albion. But after a few more monotonous minutes, all his doubts were washed away. Mercifully the ref blew up to end one of the drabbest nil-nil draws in recent history. Right away, the Albion hordes streamed on to the pitch to hoist their heroes shoulder high. In the sheer joy and relief of the moment, even Jimbo got swept up and taken on a lap of honour.

It was as if they had won the League, the FA Cup and the Charity Shield all in one go. But as Fred reached over to touch fists with Luke, the two boys knew the real score. They had stayed in the League by the skin of their teeth. But if they played against Barcelona the way they'd just played against Northampton, the fans would have to pick them up all over again afterwards – to bury them.

"I've asked you to come up here to my personal suite," squeaked Jimbo, "because I want you all to hear this news before anyone else."

The entire first-team squad, plus Benny, Ruel and Terry Vaudeville blinked. It was Wednesday morning. With the UEFA Cup Final just eight days away, everyone had arrived at the Majestic for the first training session since the Northampton game. But uniformed security men had directed them all up to Jimbo's palace-like offices instead. Now they were sitting around a huge rectangular mahogany table, staring up at Princey in his tracksuit.

"Could we make it quick then, Mr P?" asked Benny, both hands deep in his sheepskin pockets. "Terry and I have worked out a rigorous routine for the lads today. We're gonna need a full three hours to get through it before lunch."

Jimbo, at the opposite end of the table from him, smiled back strangely. "I don't think that's going to be a problem, Mr B," he said confidently.

Just then, the door opened and in walked two women. First Mrs Plunkett, who smiled sweetly at everyone, put her handbag on the table and sat down next to Princey. Right behind her came someone even older – Mrs Bowman, who had been Albion's tea-lady since 1957. After much pleading from Benny, Jimbo had allowed her to come over to the Majestic in the big move from Ash Acre.

"Ooh!" she laughed. "You're all in today, are you? What'll it be, then – tea for twenty? I won't be a jiffy." Then off she went to fetch her trolley.

Jimbo pulled himself up to his full height – about five foot four. He still had that funny little smile on his lips, but he was blinking hard behind his glasses. Luke had a cold, sick feeling in his stomach. From the way Cool F kept playing with his shades, his mate didn't look too happy about this either.

News, Jimbo had said. Whichever way Luke looked at it, he couldn't imagine it would be *good* news. But at least Terry Venables wasn't on his way in. That much was certain. On Sunday Big Tel had made a public statement that no one had approached him to take on the Albion job. And besides, he'd joked, no one else would ever be able to fill out that sheepskin coat like Benny Webb!

"Gentlemen," Jimbo announced, then he glanced down at Mrs Plunkett, "and lady. As

39

you know, all sorts of rumours have been going round recently. To do with Benny. And my plans to replace him. They're all absolute nonsense."

The players, Tel and Ruel all broke into a round of delighted applause. But Jimbo raised a hand to quieten them, then he went on: "Benny *can't* be replaced. He has done a unique job here – taking Castle Albion from the foot of the Third Division to the Final of the UEFA Cup. It's incredible." More applause, another raised hand from Jimbo. "No one could repeat such a feat. Not even the most experienced manager in the world."

But, thought Luke, putting one hand in his pocket and fiddling with those few blades of grass from Ash Acre. I know there's going to be a *but*...

"But," Jimbo went on after clearing his throat, "all good things have to come to an end. It's my belief that – in keeping us in the League – Benny has taken this club as far as he can. For that reason, Benny, I'm now letting you go."

"Letting him go?!" cried Terry, as everyone else's jaw dropped. "But he don't *wanna* go! He ain't *asked* to go! And Albion *need* him now like never before! We're in the UEFA Cup Final in a week's time!"

Jimbo flushed but still forced a smile. "I hear what you say, Terry. I've given this a great deal of thought, I can assure you. Weighed up all the pros and cons. But I do feel that it's now in the best interests of Castle Albion FC to take off in a new direction..."

"Yeah, right," snorted Ruel. "Downwards! 'Cos that's the only way we'll go without Ben. He's the soul of this club! Let him go and we die!"

Jimbo shook his head sorrowfully. "I know what a shock this must be to some of you. But I haven't got where I am today without taking tough decisions. I have big dreams for Castle Albion. A whole new ball game..."

" 'Whole new ball game' – *pah*!" spat a voice from the doorway. No one had noticed Mrs Bowman come back into the room with her tea-trolley. Now they all turned to see her fuming, hands on hips, with her eyes burning into Princey. "This isn't about dreams. It's revenge, pure and simple. You're kicking Benny out just because he kicked *you* out of the team before the semi-final in Paris! And not before time too – if you ask anyone who knows a thing about football! The only thing Ben did wrong was to let you play for so *long*!"

"Yes," said Jimbo, clearing his throat again and looking back at the players, "thank you, Mrs Bowman. I don't believe that I asked for your opinion."

"No!" Mrs Bowman ranted on. "That's half your trouble, Sonny Jim. You're far too big for your boots. You reckon you know it all and you just don't care what anyone else thinks. But listen to what *I* think, what *all* the fans think..."

"That's ENOUGH!"

Luke and everyone else jumped. But it wasn't Jimbo who'd had enough. It was Benny – standing now and buttoning up his coat. "I'm sorry for shouting, Mrs Bowman," he said much more quietly. "I appreciate what you said – and what you said too, Tel and Ruel. But if I'm not mistaken, none of this is gonna change our chairman's mind. So I think it's the best thing for everyone concerned now if I just walk away. With a bit of dignity."

He began to head for the door. "It's been great working with you, lads," he said as he went. "I wish you all the very best in Rome..."

"Hey hold on, Ben!" shouted Terry. "If you go, I go!" And up he jumped.

"I'm with you too, Boss!" said Ruel, rising and following the two of them out.

"I seriously suggest," said Jimbo to the players, "that no one else leaves this room. Not if you want to have any chance of playing in the UEFA Cup Final."

They all sat mesmerized. It was just too much to take in. Benny gone, Terry gone, Ruel gone. And they didn't even know who was going to take over yet.

Then Mrs Bowman waddled up behind

Jimbo's chair. "Well I'm not going to be playing in the UEFA Cup Final," she announced. "So *I'm* free to go! But before I do…"

She glanced at her enormous teapot, had second thoughts, picked up her milk jug, held it over Jimbo's curly head – then poured the whole lot all over him.

8

"So what did Jimbo do then?" asked Rodney – his eyes like saucers – as Luke told the story that evening in the kitchen.

"Well, there wasn't much he *could* do," said Luke. "But when Mrs Bowman reached for the sugar bowl too, Mrs Plunkett jumped up and asked her to leave. Which she did – singing: '*If you all hate Jimbo, clap your hands!*' "

"If I'd been her," snarled Luke's mum through gritted teeth, "I'd have rammed his head *in* the teapot!"

Luke winced. She never said a word without meaning it.

"But what then?" Rodney pressed Luke. "Did Jimbo say who was going to take over? There's nothing about it in the evening paper. Just that Benny is 'leaving by mutual agreement, to take his career forward in other areas'."

Luke shook his head and looked across the kitchen table. Frederick was sitting there, after coming home from school with him. (He often did. The Cool One always went *where* he wanted, *when* he wanted. He lived with his elder sister, Adele, who was his legal guardian. But as long as he kept getting straight As in school, she let him sort his own life outside it.) Frederick shrugged at Luke. He was dwelling on this thing so much, he'd ignored five calls in a row on his mobile.

"No," Luke answered. "Princey just said the meeting was over, then went to find a towel to mop up the milk. He was pretty stroppy."

"I bet he was," Rod agreed. "It's usually him handing out the stick. They say that when he was a little kid, *he* used to spank his *parents*."

"It's beyond me," said Luke. "He said that even the most experienced manager couldn't replace Benny. So why did he get rid of him?"

"Maybe he'll appoint Mrs Plunkett?" suggested Rodney, half-seriously.

"Well, we'll find out soon enough," Luke sighed. "He's coming here to see me any minute now. Cool F too, since he's here. He said on the phone he'd drop by at eight." He curled his toes in his trainers. "Apparently he needed to talk to you, Mum. Said he needed your permission for something."

"Permission to jump head-first into a teapot?" she growled, fingering her klaxon horn but deciding not to give it a blow for good measure. "And talking of cast-iron idiots, was that your father on the phone just now?"

Luke shuddered. "Um – yeah. He rang just before going on stage in New Mexico. The news about Benny hit him really hard. He's gonna try and make a window in his world tour to get back *before* the Rome game now."

"Hah! What does he think *he* can do?" his mum snorted. "Play a dopey hippie tune and get everyone to sit in a circle and hold hands?" But before Luke could answer, the doorbell rang and Rodney dashed out to answer it.

Moments later, into the kitchen stalked the Least-Gifted Player Ever To Wear An Albion Shirt. "Mrs Green!" piped Jimbo. "It's a pleasure to meet you."

"Well I'm afraid I can't say the same..." Luke's mum began, squinting up at him from the table. But she stopped in her tracks when she saw two burly minders in black suits and ties squeeze into the room too. One nodded, then the other moved the opened milk-carton out of Luke's mum's reach.

"Mrs Green," Jimbo piped on, "I'd like your permission to take Luke away for a week. Frederick too. I've cleared it with their headmistress."

"Take them?" Luke's mum gasped. Surprisingly, those minders had really got to her. Usually she didn't care who she had to tackle; and, to be fair, the minders were looking at her (and her horn) pretty nervously. "Where to?"

"Well, firstly to a luxury suite in my Majestic Village Hotel. Then on to Rome, as we build up to the big game next week. My idea is to keep all the players together, so that they can really *bond*. For a week they'll do nothing but focus on the huge task ahead – no interruptions, no distractions. What do you say?"

"Well, I…" she stuttered. Luke and Frederick looked at each other. They were both clearly thinking the same thing: a week locked up with Madman, Chrissie and Co! Now that was awesome! "Well, if everyone else is going to be there," Luke's mum blurted out, "and his headmistress says yes, then I suppose…"

"Brill!" cried Jimbo. "Go and throw a few things in a bag then, Luke. We can call in at your place on the way, Frederick. I'm sure your big sister won't have a problem with this, will she? You can call her on your mobile."

"Way to go," was all Fred said, nodding his head.

Still not altogether sure about this, Luke went upstairs and found a couple of changes of clothing. Down below, he could hear Jimbo complimenting his mum on her herbaceous borders – a sure way to get into her good books. When he came back down, everyone but Fred was standing at the kitchen window, looking out at the biggest display of garden gnomes in southern Britain.

"Er," said Luke as they all turned round, "There's just one thing, James."

"Yes," grinned the corkscrew-haired Supernerd. "What is it?"

"Well, we were all just wondering – because you didn't mention it at the meeting today... Um, who is actually going to be taking over from Benny?"

"Ah!" said Jimbo. His two minders stepped in close to him and rolled their shoulders. It was as if they expected major trouble as soon as he gave his answer. "I'd have thought that was obvious. It's going to be me! As of today I'll be trebling up – first chairman, then player, now manager. As I've told you, I have big dreams for Castle Albion. And this way, I cut down on the wage-bill too!"

Then he clapped his hands, loudly, and Luke wondered for a moment if he'd dreamed the last bit and suddenly woken up. But the looks on the faces of his mum, Rod and Fred told him otherwise. Princey really was the new Boss. "OK," he piped, leading the way out. "Let's get this show on the road!"

9

The inevitable fire-extinguisher fight broke out on the third night.

It was amazing really that Madman, Chrissie, Darius and Keatsy had held themselves back for so long. They all had their different reasons for feeling restless. Jimbo's round-the-clock curfew stopped Madman from dashing out of the Village Hotel for a hot pie every hour, on the hour. Jimbo's "No Wives, No Girlfriends" order meant that Chrissie had to spend his first-ever twenty-four hours apart from his darling fiancée Sara. The other two – diehard dance-music fans – couldn't cope with Jimbo's strict "No Speed Garage At Ear-Splitting Volume" ruling. (Luke, for his part, was quite glad to be away from his mum. She'd been regularly waking him up at night with tips on how to improve his crossing.)

So what did they do, just to let off a little steam? They stockpiled every fire-extinguisher in the plush hotel. Then at midnight they broke into the suite where Dennis and Craig were rooming together. Luke and Fred – who were sharing the suite next door – didn't actually *see* what happened next. But within moments, amid a din that sounded like a cruise missile hitting its target, a great cloud of foam started to billow out of the doorway on to the landing.

Moments after that, hooters went off all round as Jimbo's security staff swung into action. Those guys didn't mess about. They had their truncheons out even before they piled into the foam. And almost at once there was no noise *at all*.

The players poking their heads out of the other rooms looked at one another and gulped. Then Jimbo dashed out of the lift, plonking on his glasses and tying up his blue-and-white-hooped dressing-gown over his skinny bare legs.

"Don't hurt them! Don't hurt them!!" he yelled into the great mass of foam. "Don't *take* them out – just *bring* them out!!!"

Then out they were brought – one by one. Soaked through, stunned-looking, each with his arm locked behind his back by a security guy twice his size: Madman, Chrissie, Darius, Keatsy, all in tracksuits and balaclava helmets – then poor Dennis and Craig, wearing only their underpants.

"Good work, men," said Jimbo with his sternest face. "You can let them go now. I'll deal with this."

"We didn't do anything!" Craig and Dennis whined as soon as they got their arms back. "We were just minding our own business and they ... invaded us."

Jimbo shut his eyes and raised both hands. The security guys were standing in a line behind him now, making him look tinier than ever. "I don't want to hear a *thing* about who did it, or who had it done to them. This just isn't acceptable behaviour in hotel accommodation of this quality. *Is* it?"

"No," muttered all the players involved, bowing their heads.

"No – *what*?" Jimbo almost shrieked, with a stamp of his bare foot.

The players didn't look up. You could hardly hear their voices: "No ... Boss."

"That's better! It's not so very difficult, is it?" Luke wasn't so sure about that. Training for the past couple of days had consisted mainly of Jimbo (speaking by microphone from the dugout) coaching the players to call him by his "proper" title. It seemed pretty important to him. Even Mrs Plunkett had to call him Boss now. Half-Fat reckoned he'd seen a couple of blokes from Armani measuring him up for a miniature sheepskin coat too.

"I'm not happy about this, though," the mini-manager went on. "Not happy at all. I've got you all here to focus purely on football, away from the off-putting glare of intrusive media interest. *Not* to fool around with fire-extinguishers."

"But that's what footballers *do*, Boss," Keatsy pleaded. "When they're not playing or practising, there's not a lot else to get up to. Especially when you won't let us go and open supermarkets or even talk to our agent on his mobile."

This was another sore point. "There's nothing Neil Veal can do for you at present," Jimbo declared. "He's got his hands full enough." He glanced at his watch. "As we speak, he's crossing the English Channel by pedalo with one of you lot. It's not *my* fault that Dogan Mezir won't travel by train, boat or plane."

That was true enough. Dennis Bergkamp refused to fly, but shaggy old Super-Dog could get to away games only by tandem – and by pedalo too, if it was abroad. A brilliant footballer on his day, he was a simple, uneducated lad off the pitch. The only words of English he knew were *I am exceedingly pleased* (or *delighted) to meet you*. And he was sure that the throbbing engine of any form of powered transport would rip his soul right out of his muscular body.

An awkward pause followed. The players shuffled their feet. Jimbo looked at them sternly. "I only hope your noise didn't wake up Mrs Plunkett," he said. "Now I'm not quite sure what penalties to inflict on you."

"Penalties!" groaned Madman, who knew more about *them* than most. "Already we're not allowed to leave this place, or talk to anyone outside by phone, or read the newspapers, or listen to the radio or watch TV!"

"A total media blackout is the best thing you could have," Jimbo fired back. "It keeps your heads uncluttered. Keeps you focused on *football*. But ... if you're at a loose end, then I *can* let you play an early version of *VirtuAlbion*, the live-action game that I got you all to model for a few weeks ago..."

A chorus of "Cool!", "Safe!", "Spot on!" and "Nice one!" went up from a handful of the more computer-literate squad members.

"Although, of course, the players involved in this juvenile fight will *not* be given that privilege."

A new chorus of "Oh, ref!", "Come *on*!", and "That's so unfair!" went up from the Fire Extinguisher Four and the Terribly-Hard-Done-By Two. But in vain.

"That's my last word on the matter," yelled Jimbo, before stomping back off towards the lift. "If you've got any complaints, put them to my security staff."

The guys in the uniforms took one step forward. Smiling faintly, they all tapped their truncheons on the palms of their hands. "Gentlemen?" they said.

10

Training the next morning – Saturday – was no better than the two sessions before. Jimbo's ideas on getting warmed up were crazy – fifty laps of the pitch, half of them sprints. By the time they'd finished, the players were in no fit state for exercises, set-piece work or a practice game. But Jimbo put them through all that anyway, excusing himself – until the game – with that "iffy toe" again.

The new boss picked the sides. His own had four more players than the other. He also set the rules. To cut out the danger of him getting crocked, no one was allowed to come within five yards of him. Anyone who did – and was spotted by whistle-lady Mrs Plunkett – would be sent off at once. As a result, before ten minutes had passed Narris, Half-Fat, Dennis, Carl and Darius were all watching glumly from the bench. And two of them had been on Jimbo's own side.

The players still on the pitch couldn't get going. Passes went astray, tackles were mistimed, runs made in the wrong direction. Madman and Craig even started slapping each other after colliding when going for the same ball. To be honest, it was woeful. If Louis van Gaal and his Barcelona Boys had caught a glimpse of this, they would have been laughing all the way to Rome's Olympic Stadium. Surely the UEFA Cup was going to be theirs for the taking! But to Luke, at least, the oddest and most disturbing thing was *not* hearing Benny Webb go bananas every time someone did something wrong. It was creepy. Like watching *Match of the Day* without John Motson's commentary. Or wearing a pair of shorts with only one leg. Or cycling past a burger stall on match day without being hit by the stink of hot fat. Un*real*.

And here was a funny thing: none of the players had said much about Benny. Luke knew he was in their minds. So were Terry and Ruel. But something stopped them from *saying* how much they missed him, or what a horribly bad decision it had been. Quite a few of them had seen managers sacked before. It was a grisly business, and badly upsetting. But life had to go on. The next game had to be played. There was no point in crying over spilt milk (unless, of course, you were Jimbo, and you'd had it spilt all over your head).

But every time Luke now remembered the Sheepskin Supremo, he had to gulp a little bit harder. It just wasn't *right* to be going to Rome without him. It didn't make any sort of sense. Oh where, oh where was Webby now?!

"OK, that'll do!" Jimbo screeched at Mrs Plunkett, who blew her whistle for full-time. "Not a bad session, I think," the Baby Boss beamed at the seven players who had not been ordered off. "I'd say we're in pretty good shape for our match against the Premiership Select XI tomorrow afternoon."

"Yeah, right," grumbled Gaffer (who never normally grumbled). "As long as they select a side full of blokes with broken legs. We might get a draw."

The mood was pretty poor all round as the players trudged back to their five-star prison. All they had to look forward to for the rest of that day was wall-to-wall *VirtuAlbion* – and six of them were banned even from playing that. Luke and Fred walked in silence past the building site next to the hotel. This was Jimbo's latest addition to the Village – a multiplex cinema. Pretty soon, thought Luke, Jimbo would be putting up temporary market stalls on the actual pitch.

"Pssssst!" hissed a workman filling a wheelbarrow as Luke went by. He had a yellow helmet on, and the collar of his check shirt was turned up. For a moment Luke couldn't see his face clearly. Then he did.

"Grandpa!" he gasped. "What are *you* doing

here? I didn't even know you were in town."

"Never mind about that," the old boy whispered in his thick Yorkshire accent, continuing to fill the wheelie with great clods of earth. Before retiring he'd run a construction firm, so he knew how to get into these places. "I reckoned this was the only way I'd get to speak to you, lad. It's easier to break into the Tower Of London than that hotel your new manager's keeping you in."

"But what is it?" Luke whispered back. "Is something wrong? Something I should know about?" His thoughts flew to the person most likely to have got into a mess of some kind. "It's not Dad, is it?"

"No, lad, no. He's doing fantastic. Sell-out concerts wherever he goes. And the album's already gone platinum in seventeen different countries. No, it's not TAFKAG. It's Benny."

"How so?" asked Cool F.

"Well, it's *about* Benny. The fans are putting on a huge campaign to bring him back. Thousands of them are camped day and night outside Ash Acre – as a protest at him being fired. There's going to be a march through town tomorrow afternoon, while you're playing that Premiership lot here behind closed doors. That's why Jimbo's not letting you have any contact with the outside world, you see. He doesn't want you to know about any of it."

"Whew!" breathed Luke. "I wish Fred and I

could be on that march. Or at least get over to Ash Acre. Then we could tell all the fans we agree with them."

"Aye lad, you haven't got a prayer in the UEFA Cup Final with Princey managing you, or – pity help us – playing. Everyone knows that."

"Except the man himself," murmured Frederick. "Could he use a reality check!"

Luke's Grandpa nodded sadly. "Look, there's got to be some way round this. Some sort of solution. We've all got to put our heads together. But I'll tell you this: if you could somehow get over to Ash Acre after the game tomorrow it would do the fans a power of good. If they knew you *players* wanted Benny back too, the campaign would really take off..."

"Oi, you there!" came a shriek from outside the hotel. "In the yellow helmet! Get on with your work and stop wasting my players' time!" It was Jimbo, looking pretty suspicious. "What are you talking about, anyway?"

Quickly Grandpa pulled a bus ticket and a biro out of his pocket and thrust it into Luke's hand. "Just asking for the young chaps' autographs, sir!" he called back. And as both boys pretended to scribble their names, he added under his breath, "Do what you can tomorrow, lads. We've got to get this sorted... Oh, and Luke, your mum says you'd *better* be working on your first-time lay-offs."

11

"What's wrong with Jimbo?!" said Craig Edwards, gaping. "Doesn't he *like* us?! Doesn't he want us to *live* till next Thursday night?!!!"

The Albion squad had just run out into the empty Majestic Stadium, to find the Premiership Select XI already kicking in. Kicking footballs, that was – not kicking one another. But just about all these boys knew how to put the boot in. It must have cost Albion's player-manager-chairman a small fortune to get them to turn up for a mere practice match. But he'd kept their identities a secret until now. And Luke and Co immediately saw why. It was terrifying!

In goal was Shaka Hislop, which was fair enough. He was *big*, for sure, but no one had ever accused him of putting himself about. Then there was his defence: Neil Ruddock, Matt Elliott, Jaap Stam and Martin Keown. Four centre-halves! But what they lacked in mobility, they more than made up for in muscle.

And who was going to be strung across

midfield? None other than Dennis Wise, Paul Ince, Roy Keane and Lee Bowyer – tasty in the tackle, or what? And to round things off up front, there was a two-man strike force of Tough Cookie Robbie Fowler and Duncan "Disorderly" Ferguson.

"I don't feel very well," whimpered Chrissie.

"Who's their manager for the day?" said Gaffer. "Vinnie Jones?!"

"How could this lot ever play in a 'friendly' against anyone?" asked Darius. "We're gonna look like a bunch of Carl's used pineapples by the end!"

A smile began to spread over Narris's face. "Hey," he said in a low voice. "But *this* mob aren't gonna stay five yards away from Jimbo, are they? They'll have him for breakfast! Lads, it looks as if our prayers will be answered."

"I'm not so sure about that," sighed Madman. "Look." He nodded at the tunnel.

Two figures in three-piece suits were walking out into the hazy May sunshine. One was little Princey. The other – twirling what looked like a shotgun in one hand – was the Premiership XI's manager. Was it…? It *was*! Vinnie Jones!!!

It wasn't a shooter, though. Just a shooting stick – for Vinnie to sit on near the touchline and bark instructions at his boys for the rest of the afternoon. Jimbo came over to the Albion squad with a very slight limp.

"The old toe started playing up again when I was about to get changed," he explained. "So I decided to give today's game a miss. It's nothing *too* serious. But if I'm going to be in peak condition on Thursday, I ought to give it a rest."

"Right, Boss," Keatsy said forlornly. "We'd hate you to miss the Final."

Jimbo frowned at him, not quite sure if he was serious. Then Carl cut in: "That's not a bad side you've found to play against us, Boss."

"Yes," Jimbo agreed, trotting over to the dug-out. "I wanted you to have a stern test. See what you're made of against top-quality opposition. I'll be watching *very* closely. And remember – I haven't yet made my final decision on who will be in the team on Thursday. There's everything to play for!"

But oddly – as it turned out – there wasn't very much to play *against*. However much Vinnie and Jimbo roared and screeched from the line to "get stuck in" and "mix it a bit", none of the players really did. The Premiership boys had just finished a gruelling season and weren't really in the mood to take no prisoners. Also, they weren't stupid. None of them wanted to clatter an Albion player just before the biggest game of his entire career. So the game was played at half-pace, there was hardly any physical contact, and no one even scored a goal.

But there was one more reason why the

visitors weren't playing it the way Jimbo wanted. Luke found out about it when guest-ref Paul Alcock blew for full-time, and all the players shook hands before leaving the pitch.

"What Princey did to Benny Webb was all wrong," said Shaka Hislop as he stooped to high- (or low-) five the Studless Sensation. "Us guys think it was well out of order. We're a hundred per cent behind the fans on this one. Big Ben should get his job back. I was even planning on looking in at Ash Acre myself afterwards. To show maximum support, y'know?"

Frederick pricked up his ears at that. "Hey, big fella," he said to the gentle giant of a goalie. "You wouldn't happen to have a big bag for your kit?"

"You bet," grinned Shaka. "I carry so much stuff around with me, I use two."

"Sorted," nodded Cool F. He obviously had a cunning plan.

Then he leaned in closer, and explained to Luke and Shaka just what it was.

12

Shaka Hislop strode out of the Majestic Stadium, calling goodbye to Martin Keown and Robbie Fowler. Draped round his neck was a blue-and-white-hooped scarf. Not an Albion one, but a relic from his mid-90s glory days with Reading.

Lugging two huge leather bags, he headed for his people carrier. Anyone watching him would have thought he was talking to himself: "Not far now... Just a few steps more..." He opened the back and carefully stashed the two bags side by side. Then, before shutting the boot, he unzipped both: "Just to give you a bit more air in there..."

He drove away, but only as far as the T-junction with the main road into town. "The coast's clear," he shouted into the back of his vehicle. "You can come out now." And grinning, Luke and Frederick clambered out of the bags. "Escape from Alcatraz, eh?" chortled Shaka. "Ash Acre, here we come!"

It took a while to get to the old ground. The protest march through town had clearly been a big one. Police diversion signs were up everywhere – not to mention plenty of boys in blue themselves, lots of them on horses. But what Luke and Frederick *didn't* understand was the sight of hundreds and hundreds of pairs of pants littering the roads and pavements. Every shape, size and colour. Jockey shorts, Y-fronts, women's frilly knickers. What was all *that* about?

"The media boys will have gone home by now," said Shaka as he accelerated up Cranham Hill, with creaky old Ash Acre's floodlights poking up behind it. "That's good for you. You don't want Jimbo hearing about you being here. Oh and look, you guys, take a pair of pants each out of my bags. I brought plenty."

"*Pants?*" asked Luke and Frederick, holding up some gigantic boxers between them.

"It's a Pants Protest," Shaka grinned. "The fans think that what Jimbo did to Benny was absolute pants." He buzzed down his window, and the unmistakable sound of Rocky Mitford and the South Side Chorus filled the people carrier:

"If you all want Benny, flash your pants!
If you all want Benny, flash your pants!
If you all want Benny, all want Benny,
All want Benny,
If you all want Benny, flash your pants!"

Luke felt a tingle run up his spine. I'm coming back home, he thought. There was even the disgusting reek of Ash Acre's very own brand of ghastly-burgers! Then they turned into the players' and officials' car park – and Luke caught his breath as he saw the huge encampment of the Castle Albion Massive. It was like a medieval army. But instead of flags and banners flying everywhere, there were more pairs of pants than you could shake a forestful of sticks at.

In the old days, you could get only about 12,000 people into Ash Acre. There must have been twice that number outside it now, spilling right over into the nearby public park. Everywhere Luke looked there were sheets and blankets hanging from trees and from the windows of Ash Acre.

James Prince is a Royal Pain! said the writing on one.

Bring Back Our Benny! said many others.

P is for PRINCE. P is for PRAT. P is for PANTS! said a *lot* more.

By now so many fans had flocked around Shaka's vehicle that he switched off the engine and put on his handbrake. "Shaka! It's Shaka Hislop!!" people were shouting. And then, much louder: "He's got Luke and Frederick in there! Luke and Frederick are here!!"

As the two local heroes climbed out, *such* a cheer went up. If the fans had all been crammed inside Ash Acre, the din would probably have blown the roof off. (But then again, the roof in there had been close to caving in for years.)

"Luke! Fred!" called the loudest voice in football fandom: Rocky Mitford, in his Seventies replica shirt and what looked like a tiny replica of himself on his shoulders – his six-year-old daughter, Polly. "You're here! How'd you get out!"

"With difficulty!" Luke yelled at him over the crowd's chants. "And Shaka's gonna have to take us straight back – before Jimbo misses us. But we just wanted to show we're right behind you. We want Benny back too!"

Cool F hoisted Shaka's pants high above his head and gave them a twirl.

"Yesssssss!"
roared the fans, followed by a quick burst of:
"He's Black, He's Cool,
He Kicks It Like A Mule:
Freddie D! Freddie D!"

Then several dozen kids did an action replay of Frederick's rocket shot against Hull. Cool F saluted them with such a complicated set of hand movements, it was going to take his devoted young fans the rest of the week to learn them off by heart.

"Listen, Rocky," cried Luke, looking all round the encampment, and spotting his Nan and Grandpa waving from a distant tent. "Where's Benny himself? What's he doing? Has he been here at all?"

Rocky shook his big curly head. And Little Polly shook her head too. "No one's seen him since the day Jimbo fired him," Rocky said. "There's all sorts of rumours. They say the job offers are flooding in: Milan, Celtic, Blackburn, Wales, the United Arab Emirates..."

"Wow! He's not going to *take* one, is he?"

Rocky and Polly did a double shrug. "Let's hope not. But we're about ninety per cent sure he's going to come here tomorrow night. Tel and Ruel too."

"*And* Mrs Bowman!" Polly reminded him, with a hard tap on the head.

"Yeah, her too," Rocky grinned. "It would be so great if you two – and some of the rest of the lads – could get over here then. We could work out a proper plan of campaign together. Try and get this horrible mess sorted once and for all."

Luke looked at Frederick. "Well, we'll try. But it won't be easy." At that, Shaka started up his engine again, looked at the boys and tapped his watch. "We've gotta go, Rocky. But we'll do whatever we can – that's a promise. OK?"

"*O-K!*" boomed Rocky. "Just give Jimbo one from us!"

"One what?" asked Luke, clambering back up into the four-wheeler.

"I'll leave *that* to your imagination! Oh Albion! Al-bee-YON!"

"Albion! Albion!
AL-BEE-YON!"

13

That night, Luke and Fred broke the silence at the hotel about Benny Webb. In Gaffer's room they told the other players about the Pants Protest. They all listened in wonder – especially to the bit about Benny's job offers.

"The United Arab Emirates!" whistled Half-Fat. "That's in the desert. The Boss would *melt* in his sheepskin coat out there!"

The others gazed at him. Not because of the joke he'd made. But because he had called Benny "The Boss". Which was, of course, just the way that all the others still thought of him.

Jimbo might *call* himself by that name. He might make the squad do the same. He might even get himself a sheepskin. But for this group of players, there was only one man who had their respect. One man whose bellowing and gesturing meant anything to them, even if it made no real sense to anyone else. Benny Webb wasn't just their true manager. He was like their *dad*. (Why else did he call every single one of them "son"?) And even if your dad can sometimes be the world's most enormous prannit, you can't stop being – well – his kids.

For a few moments the players sat in silence. Then Gaffer spoke up. "All right, then," he said. "So what are we going to do?"

"*Do?*" asked Narris. "Isn't it obvious? We've got to get him back. The fans want it. We want it."

Everyone nodded. But Dennis also pulled a face. "The trouble is – fans and players don't generally choose their own manager, do they? Especially if the bloke they want to get rid of also happens to be the chairman."

"Sad but true," Carl agreed. "And Jimbo's put so much dosh into this club. The way he sees it – he's paid off all Albion's debts, and given us this brand new stadium, so he's earned the right to manage the team. After giving Benny the boot, he's not just gonna stand aside and let him come back now, is he?"

Luke shrugged. He couldn't stop thinking about all those loyal fans at Ash Acre. He couldn't stop thinking about Ash Acre either. Again he dipped a hand into his pocket and ran the dried-up blades of grass through his fingers. It had been weird to go back there with Shaka. So many people had said so many harsh things about the old ground. And yes, it wasn't anywhere near as spectacular as the Majestic. It didn't have shiny blue seats on all four sides. It didn't even have a roof on two of them. And it stank of old onions and Bovril, and there were birds nesting in the rafters of the main stand, and it didn't have a PA system that worked... And yet, it still seemed like home. It still seemed like the kind of place where Castle Albion *belonged*, where they'd had so much Cup success in recent times, with the fans only an arm's length away from the touchline – not just behind the team but *with* it, almost a *part* of it.

"No," said Cool F, in answer to Carl's question. "JP won't just say, 'Hey, Ben, welcome back.' We've gotta give the dude no option."

"Give him no option?" asked Craig. "How?"

"Well, that's what we'd have to discuss with Rocky and the fans tomorrow night," said Luke, finding his voice again, "and maybe Benny too."

"First we'd have to break out of this place," Chrissie pointed out. "How could we get past those security guys? They're on duty right through the night."

Luke reached into his other pocket and produced a bulky envelope.

"What's that?" asked Casper. "Money to bribe them with?"

"Better than money." Luke took out a wad of tickets. "These things are like a licence to *print* money. Tickets for my dad's Rome gig after the UEFA Final!"

"With all due respect," said Dennis, "will those goons really want an earful of your dad? I mean, they won't be up for all that flower-power stuff, will they?"

"Probably not," Luke smiled. "But this is the hottest gig in music right now. There are punters around with more money than sense who would *die* for tickets. So the goons could make a small fortune flogging them off – right?"

"Riiiiiiight," said everyone, slowly nodding their heads.

"Dad gave them to me on the stadium's opening day. He said I was to hand them out to you lot, as a surprise, after we'd beaten Barcelona. But I reckon if we let those goons have them, they'll turn a blind eye to us going walkabout."

Everyone nodded faster – partly, no doubt, in relief at avoiding the gig themselves.

"So look," Luke went on, "as soon as Jimbo's safely tucked up in bed tomorrow night, we'll meet again in here. Then we'll go and see some muscle men about some tickets. Right?"

"Right!" agreed everyone.

"And do we all have to bring extra pants?" asked Craig. "To wave around?"

"You bet!" cried Darius. "All except Madman. He's only got the one pair!"

14

Getting out of the hotel was as easy as Dwight Yorke stroking the ball into an empty net. The security goons just nodded, pocketed the TAFKAG concert tickets, then waved Luke and the rest of the squad through to freedom.

"They didn't seem to care whether Jimbo found out," said Dennis as they ran for the first bus into town. "If he did, he'd surely sack them all on the spot."

"They'd probably be relieved," Craig replied. "They must hate working for him just as much as we do. I reckon one was a TAFKAG fan on the quiet, too."

Since it was so late, there was no one else on the bus. The streets looked pretty deserted too. But as soon as they got close to Ash Acre, all that changed. The encampment had grown even bigger since Luke and Fred's visit the day before. Hordes of fans were now stretched out in sleeping bags on the grass verges at the top of Cranham Hill. There were even twenty tents on the big roundabout next to the park. High above them, thousands of pairs of pants had been stitched together and pegged on a washing-line between two lampposts to spell out the simple patchwork message:

WE WANT WEBB!

"This is amazing!" breathed Gaffer as the bus pulled in at the Ash Acre stop. "I didn't know we *had* so many fans!"

"And I didn't know they had so many pants!" murmured Madman.

"It's all so *quiet*," marvelled Casper, getting off the bus.

"You're right," whispered Chrissie in front of him. "There's so many people – and look, there are masses of them over there by the ground who are wide awake – yet they're hardly making a sound!"

"I guess they can't afford to cause any sort of disturbance," said Half-Fat, looking both ways before crossing the road, "especially at night, or else the police would make them all go home."

"Hey!" said Darius hoarsely. "Isn't that Terry's blue Metro pulling in by the South Side turnstiles? And who's that in front with him?"

"It's the Boss!"

erupted from just about all the others in a top-volume chorus that turned thousands of heads in the players' and officials' car park. And that's just who it was! The hero had come home!

Benny Webb – hauling himself out of the small car and stiffly straightening up before taking a long look round.

Meanwhile, tracksuited Terry got out of the driver's side, turned around, and helped first Ruel Bibbo and then Mrs Bowman out of the back. Everyone was moved to see them too. But soon all eyes were back on Ben.

He looked calm, noble, craggy, almost mythic. A king returned from exile – white-bearded and bright-eyed in the darkness – back now among his most loyal supporters as they flooded silently around him, reaching out in joy and wonder just to touch the hem of his sheepskin.

He saluted them all, but when the players approached, he gave each one a hug like a long-lost son. These were highly emotional moments. When Luke went to get his cheek crushed against Benny's Paisley-patterned tank-top, he felt very close to tears – and not just because the Boss was holding him so tight.

Clearly the emotion was getting to Benny too. A sea of faces looked his way, expecting words of wisdom, a rallying cry, an epic statement of his determination to lead them into the Promised Land of UEFA Cup glory. But with one hand still on Luke's shoulder, and the other on Cool F's, all he could do was swallow hard, several times. Benny Webb wasn't often struck speechless. But this was one of those rare occasions.

Yet behind every truly great manager is a truly great Number Two. A guy who knows exactly how to get things sorted when the main man is "taking a moment". So up stepped ever-trusty Terry Vaudeville. He could usually talk the hind legs off a donkey too. But he didn't need to talk. Instead he produced from behind his back ... a brand, spanking-new white leather football!

At once every single fan and player understood. This was true inspiration. A gesture of pure genius. Long ago, Moses had parted the Red Sea. Now Terry Vaudeville managed to part the ocean of fans in the players' and officials' car park. Not only that. Without any instruction, they also pressed themselves back to make a completely clear, square playing-area.

By that time, the players had peeled apart into two teams. One set of players trotted down to the far end of the square where Rocky Mitford was setting down two piles of coats for goalposts. The others stayed where they were, as Luke and Fred stacked up another set of coat-posts. Then Benny strode into the centre of the "pitch", taking the ball from Terry as he passed.

He didn't actually *say* "Let there be light!" but that was clearly what he wanted. And within a split-second, several thousand switched-on cigarette lighters were being held aloft – casting just enough of a warm glow for play to begin.

Benny tossed the ball high into the air. As it came down, Carl and Keatsy jumped high to challenge each other for it. Game on!

They didn't play for long. Fifteen minutes at the most. It was too risky to play for much longer on that cracked and weedy bit of tarmac. But what a fifteen minutes it was! On the Majestic Stadium's rolling lawn not one of these players had ever shown such a sure touch, such invention or technique.

Goals rained in from both sides, but the quality of the build-up play was just as breathtaking. From start to finish, the watching fans made one long purr of delight. They didn't want to drown out Benny's stream of comments from the "centre-spot" as the game progressed. A warning here to Narris not to dive into tackles, a suggestion there to Chrissie that he pulled a bit wider, a reminder to Keatsy that there was no law against him using his left foot, some advice to Gaffer to play the ball short from the back...

Luke could *feel* a new force flowing through both teams. One that Jimbo would never be able to tap. Benny was less like a manager here than the conductor of an orchestra. And a very fine orchestra too. The kind of orchestra that just might be able to play its way to victory in Rome against Great Big Barcelona.

"That was absolute *magic*!" grinned Rocky

when it was over, in the softest voice he was capable of. "You've *got* to come back, Benny. It's plain for all to see: you're what makes this side work. The lads can only do it for you."

Luke and the others all nodded. Rocky was right. They didn't just play for Albion. They played for Benny. He had to be there in Rome. He *had* to.

But Mr Irreplaceable sadly shook his shaggy head as he headed back to Terry's car. "I'm really touched by everything that you and your boys are doin', Rocky," he called over his shoulder. "And of course I'll be in Rome to watch the game. I wouldn't miss it for the world. But I can't just march in and claim my job back. However much you protest, Jimbo won't listen, will he?"

He waved before getting back into the car with Tel, Ruel and Mrs B. It was awful to see him going again. Truly awful. There wasn't a dry eye in the players' and officials' car park. Luke felt a crack in his voice as he said to Gaffer: "Benny's right. Jimbo won't listen to the fans. This is down to *us*."

"Us?" asked Gaffer. "What can *we* do? We're flying to Italy tomorrow."

Luke nodded slowly, watching Terry's Metro pull out into the road. "I think..." he said with great uncertainty, "I *think* I've just had an idea..."

15

Luke knew his idea was *way* risky. He said nothing more about it until the squad was winging its way to a small private airfield to the south of Rome.

Jimbo wasn't going to risk touching down at Fiumicino or Ciampino airports like any regular member of the public. The media would be waiting there in their masses – not to mention great gangs of travelling Albion fans with pants on their heads and "Bring Back Benny!" on their lips. He didn't want the squad mixing with any ordinary punters on the flight either. So they all flew over in one of his own personal jets.

In one way this was good: there was leg-room to spare for big guys like Carl and Gaffer, and the seats were a *lot* more luxurious than anything Luke had flown on before. But in another way it was bad. Because when Jimbo got an urgent business e-mail from Geneva soon after take-off, there was nothing to stop him from telling the pilot to stop over in Switzerland on the way.

"Sorry about this, lads," he grinned before hopping off the plane clutching his electronic briefcase. "I won't be more than a couple of hours. This is too good a chance for me to miss. I can buy up a big rival company before tea-time!"

"We're delighted for you," muttered Half-Fat, slumping deeper into his seat behind the *Shoot!* annual he was reading.

"Don't get in the way of any incoming aeroplanes, will you?" growled Dennis in an even lower voice and – out of Jimbo's sight – with his fingers crossed.

"I *would* ask Doris to get you all on to the correct spiritual plane for the game while I'm gone," Jimbo went on. "But sadly she always knocks herself out with sleeping pills in her own cabin during flights. I'd be grateful if you didn't wake her up with any stupid messing about." He winked. "*Ciao* for now."

"*Ciao* to you too!" grunted Narris when he was gone. "Two hours! Well, I'm not going to watch *Toy Story 2* again. Hasn't he got any other films on board?"

"We don't need films," said Gaffer softly, waving to everyone to gather round. "Luke's got an idea, and I reckon it's about time he shared it with us all."

"Oh, can't it wait?" cried Madman. "I was just

getting the hang of this. And you know what they say – when in Rome, do as the Romans do!" Ever since take-off, he had been in training for the first spaghetti meal he would eat in Italy. Mrs Plunkett had lent him a ball of wool, and now he was practising picking up long strands in the proper Italian style – with a spoon and a fork.

"Forget about food for a minute," Gaffer barked at him. "Get over here now."

"So what's the big deal?" Carl asked Luke when everyone was within whispering distance, ears agog.

"OK," said Luke, still far from sure about this, but feeling he might explode if he kept it to himself any longer. "We all want Benny back as Boss, right?"

"*Right!*"

"And we all know Jimbo won't take any notice of the fans' Pants Protest?"

"Right..."

"So it's up to *us* to twist Jimbo's arm, isn't it?"

Everyone frowned. "Yeah, but how?" asked Chrissie. "Stamp our feet and scream till he gives in?"

"No," said Luke, tilting his head and fingering a few blades of Ash Acre grass in his pocket. "Not stamp our feet. Not, in fact, move our feet *in any way at all*."

"Oh right," laughed Craig. "We're footballers, in case you've forgotten. Moving our feet is what we *do*. That's our job. Running, kicking, all that stuff."

"Which is precisely what I want us *not* to do," Luke said calmly. "I want us to go on strike. Refuse to kick a ball till JP gives in and brings back Benny – oh, and stands down from the team as well."

A chorus of gasps, snorts and "what-are-you-ons?" met that. But Luke could see Gaffer chewing this over thoughtfully and the skipper was the man who mattered here. If *he* said yes, no one else was likely to say no.

"Jimbo'll *never* give in to that sort of blackmail," said Keatsy. "You know what kind of bloke he is. He's not normal. He'd probably just say, 'OK, you lot can do what you like, I'll play Barcelona on my own!'"

Gaffer was nodding now. "It wouldn't be easy," he agreed. "At first, yeah, he might go ballistic. But I reckon in the end he might come round. And let's face it – what else can we do? With Jimbo in the team, and without Benny on the bench, we've got a one in five million chance of winning the Final – tops."

"Recognize," drawled Cool Fred. "Let's go with my man Luke. What have we got to lose?"

The other players looked at him but said nothing. *What have we got to lose?* His question seemed go round and round inside the aircraft. A question to which none of them, at that moment, could have dreamed the eventual answer.

"Are we all in on this, then?" Gaffer asked as the silence lengthened.

Most of the players shrugged. One or two nodded. Some just kept staring dead ahead. But no one said "Count me out".

"Right then," said Gaffer firmly. "Thanks for your input there, Studless. You always were the brains behind this outfit. Now here's what I suggest we do…"

16

They call Rome the Eternal City. Founded by Romulus (of Romulus and Remus fame), built on seven hills, it is the home of the Pope, pizzas, and the maddening parp-parp-parp of mopeds at all hours of the day and night. Rome the Beautiful. Rome the Historic. Rome the Religious.

But as far as the Castle Albion squad was concerned, they could have spent the past twenty-four hours in Rocky Mitford's basement. They hadn't seen a *thing* of the Vatican City, the Spanish Steps or the Sistine Chapel. Jimbo had organized this expedition like a military operation. No, not like one. It *was* one. He'd even hired a small private army of policemen to guard the players' every move.

As soon as the jet touched down at the airfield, the armed *carabinieri* hustled the squad into a fleet of limos with smoked-glass windows and escorted them directly to their riverside hotel. This was, to be fair, a pretty sumptuous top-of-the-range place to bed down in. But no player was allowed to leave the whole top floor, which Jimbo had block-booked. Just to make sure, the squaddie boys stood sentry at all the lift doors and at the tops of all the staircases. And Luke had no more TAFKAG tickets to sweeten *them* up with.

"It's all for your own good," Jimbo told them after dinner, before turning in for the night himself. "I don't want the media hacks and *paparazzi* on your backs. This way, you get to concentrate only on your mission here: the Italian Job!"

The players looked at him dubiously. Some of them had wanted to hit him that night with their strike demands. Gaffer had said no. They had to confront Jimbo on the very day before the game – tomorrow. Just before they were meant to start training at the Olympic Stadium. That would catch Princey completely unawares – and maybe even shock him into giving in at once.

"My men will deliver you to the stadium at ten hundred hours in the morning," Jimbo went on, nodding at a couple of gunslingers. (At once they clicked their heels and stood up straighter. "Yes, *Il Principe*," they said together.) "I myself have a breakfast meeting with several Italian Internet companies. So I'll travel separately, but I'll see you all on the pitch – ten o'clock sharp."

When he'd gone, everyone rolled their eyes. "Business, business, business," sighed Half-Fat. "I'm amazed he's got time to fit in a piddly game of football."

Gaffer looked at him. "Well, after tomorrow, let's hope he won't have to."

For quite a few of the players, tomorrow took a long time coming. Luke, for one, hardly slept at all. He'd started to fret about the showdown up ahead. Jimbo wasn't going to be a pushover. Right from the start he'd known about the Pants Protest, and that hadn't shaken him at all. If anything, it had seemed to make him *more* determined to do things his way. A squad of stroppy soccer players probably wouldn't have any effect on him either. And Luke felt especially bad about that. The strike was, after all, his idea. He felt *responsible*.

No one said much in the limos that ferried them the short way from the hotel to the Olympic Stadium. They were smuggled straight into the bowels of the magnificent building, bypassing all the media vultures and vulturesses. Mrs Plunkett was waiting inside with her usual big smile and even bigger handbag.

"James told me to escort you to the dressing-room," she told them. "He's already out on the pitch. Ooh, it's a lovely big one, you know! They had the 1960 Olympic Games here. And the 1990 World Cup. What a venue!"

The squad followed her through a maze of corridors to the spotless room where their training kit was laid out ready for them. "I'll go and tell James you're all here safe and sound," Mrs P beamed at them. "He can't wait to put you through your paces!" She winked. "He's really *dressed* for the part now too!"

"What's she on about?" asked Dennis when she'd disappeared.

"Never mind her," Gaffer said sternly, sitting down on the bench, crossing his legs and folding his arms. "Come on, lads. You know what you've got to do."

And they did. So they did it. Which was absolutely *nothing*. Like Gaffer, they just sat down in their everyday clothes – and waited. No undressing, no putting-on of kit, no pulling-on of boots or trainers. When old-time workers went on strike, they laid down their tools. The players of Castle Albion FC had no tools to lay down, as such. So they just sat. And they waited.

And they waited. They'd expected Jimbo to come storming in if they were even a couple of minutes late. Then they would let him know the score. But ten minutes passed. Twelve. Fifteen! Quite a few of the players started to fidget.

"Cor," said Narris, "those Christians over at the Colosseum must have felt like this – hanging about before they got sent out to meet the lions!"

"No, Narris," Darius reminded him. "*We're* the lions. Jimbo's got to meet *us*!"

And at that moment, the dressing-room door swang open. Gently. Not with a crash, bang, wallop. And in walked an odd-looking Jimbo. *Really* odd-looking.

First off, he was wearing a boy's designer version of Benny's sheepskin coat. Unreal! Second, he was smiling. Third, he didn't seem *at all* surprised to find nobody changed. Without a word he met one player's eye after another.

"So..." he said finally, thrusting both hands into deep sheepskin pockets.

Gaffer took a deep breath. "OK, Mr Prince," he began. Here came the speech that he'd practised on all the others the night before. "This is nothing against you personally, but we've decided to take industrial action. We – that's all of us here – refuse to kick another ball for Castle Albion unless Benny Webb comes back as manager – and you pack in playing for us too. Basically, that's it."

Now it was Jimbo's turn to take a breath. Luke took one too. A big one. And deep in *his* pocket he fingered his blades of Ash Acre grass for luck. Jimbo was still smiling. But instead of speaking, he just looked at each player in turn again, nodding his head slowly. That was too much for Gaffer, who couldn't help going on:

"Look, Mr P, we know this isn't how you wanted it to be. We're really sorry we've had to do it. But we know all about the Pants Protest and everything. There are thousands of loyal Albion fans who want Benny back, and for you to be just chairman. Albion *needs* Benny. And it needs you too – but only in the boardroom. You're a brilliant *chairman*. We all think that, don't we lads?"

"Oh, *yeah*! *Right! Absolutely!*" everyone burst out. But Jimbo raised a small hand to silence them. *Still* he was smiling.

"Right then," he said, "I'll keep this brief. Let me get this straight: you'll stay on strike unless a) I bring Benny back, and b) I stand down from the team?"

Looking a bit sheepish, everyone nodded.

"And I guess you want Terry, Ruel and Mrs Bowman back too?" JP grinned.

"Well … ye-e-es," everyone agreed. This was going *way* too easily.

Jimbo nodded. "I see." He nodded again.

Luke's toes were almost dropping off with the tension. *Please*, he was praying to the God of Football, *please* let this work…

Jimbo looked at his watch. "Right," he said at last – as calmly as Nigel Martyn plucks inswinging corners out of the air, "here's what I'm prepared to offer you in return. I'll give you all until noon tomorrow – match-day – to pull yourselves together. If, by that time, you are still trying to blackmail me in this way, I will quite simply pull the plug on your precious Castle Albion FC."

"Pull the plug?" cried Chrissie. "What d'you mean?"

Jimbo smiled sweetly at him. "I'll take out all the millions I've invested in the club. All the money that I spent to pay off its old debts. I'll bankrupt the club. Put it out of business. In one fell swoop, Castle Albion will cease to exist. And I'll make sure it happens *before* the UEFA Cup Final."

"But... But..." Gaffer stammered. "The club... The fans... Our dreams..."

"You should have thought about all that before," said Jimbo with a shrug.

"But the Majestic Stadium..." Dennis gasped.

"Oh, I'll hang on to that," said Jimbo, turning on his heel. "I can easily turn it into an ice-rink. As I've said: you have till noon tomorrow." Then he was gone.

What have we got to lose? Fred had asked. Now they all knew.

17

The next hour wasn't the happiest one the Albion players had ever spent. In fact, to be fair, being turned over 1-7 at home by Chesterfield had been miles more enjoyable.

They managed to smuggle themselves unnoticed out of the Olympic Stadium. (That, at least, was a relief. The *last* thing they needed now was the media dogging their every move.) But then they found themselves on the sun-kissed, tourist-crowded banks of the River Tiber without a clue what to do next.

No limos were waiting for them. They had no money, no maps, and Madman had nothing to snack on. Everything was back in their hotel. But where, exactly, was that? And what was it even *called*?

"The Garibaldi," announced Cool F. "That's what it said on the towels." He hip-swayed over to a nearby ice-cream vendor and asked him fluently where the hotel was. The guy pointed a cone southwards and back came Frederick.

"This way, brothers," he said, setting off with the rest of the squad in tow.

"I didn't know you spoke Italian," Luke said to him.

"I don't," Fred replied. "I just tried updating a bit of Latin, y'know?"

But that was the only good break the players got. The guards were standing to attention in the foyer, but not – this time – to keep the media out. When Gaffer tried to cross to the desk to pick up all their room keys, the whole unit stepped up to bar their way. The desk clerk stalked up behind them, and asked if any of the players spoke Italian. Fred tried another burst of updated Latin.

"What did he say?" asked Carl when their brief chat was over.

Frederick raised an eyebrow. "We're no longer guests here. Jimbo's orders."

"But all our stuff!" cried Madman. "I've got fifteen cans of baked beans up in my room, and a job lot of Mars Bars!"

"The whole lot's in storage now," Frederick told them.

"And my lucky cuddly donkey!" moaned Dennis. "But when can we get it all?"

"According to what Jimbo told the desk dude: 'When we decide to play ball.'"

"Or when we agree to *his* blackmail," said Craig through gritted teeth. "What kind of a person *is* he? He doesn't deserve to own a Club biscuit, let alone a football club!"

"A Club biscuit!" sighed Madman. "What I wouldn't give for six of those..."

"Look," growled Gaffer, "let's forget about food, shall we? We've got to think fast now. Act fast too. Let's get out of this place." With that, he turned and led the way back on to the street, then set off towards the city centre. Everyone else dutifully trotted along behind him. He *was* the skipper.

"But what on earth can we do?" asked Darius. "Go to St Peter's and pray? Jimbo's got all the cards in his hands, hasn't he?"

Gaffer's eyes narrowed as he swerved to avoid two nuns. "At this stage – yes."

"What's that supposed to mean?" said Craig, puffing up alongside him.

"I think I know," put in Narris. "Somehow we've got to get the cards *out* of Jimbo's hands – right?"

"Yeah," agreed Keatsy. "And put them in somebody else's, right?"

"Can someone tell me what cards we're talking about here?" pleaded Carl "What's-The-Score?" Davey, who always liked to have things spelled out as clearly as possible.

Gaffer stopped in his tracks just as he came to a big road: the Viale Giuseppe Mazzini. With the traffic blaring by behind him, he turned to face the rest.

"We've got only one hope, lads," he announced. "As long as Jimbo's in charge, nothing's ever gonna be right. Nothing's *really* been right ever since he took over. OK, he saved our bacon and stopped us from going bust. But after that, it's been one big ego-trip for him. He doesn't care about Albion. To him it's just a business like all his others. That's why he *would* pull the plug at noon tomorrow. He doesn't care about the fans, the players, the club's traditions…"

"So what are you *saying*?" Carl begged him to explain.

"*He's saying*," said every single other player, "*that we need a new owner!*"

"Oh right," said Carl, glancing at his watch. "So we've got about twenty-four hours to find ourselves one. It's a bit short notice, isn't it? Where do we start?"

At that point Cool F, who had been looking away down the busy road, nodded at a slowly-approaching bicycle built for two. "With him," he drawled.

The guy at the front of the tandem was dark-skinned, shaggy-haired, with vast glistening thighs. Dogan Mezir, Albion's number nine! The one behind was thinner, paler and a whole lot tireder-looking. But this was the chap Frederick was nodding at: Mr Neil Veal – agent to the stars! If anyone could whip out an address book, ring up a mega-millionaire and ask him to buy a football club, it was Vealo. The players let out a huge whoop of welcome.

But he *had* just travelled all the way from England to Rome by pedalo and pedal-bike. Which was why, when the tandem at last pulled up alongside the squad, he keeled right over and collapsed into the arms of Gaffer and Narris.

18

Vealy didn't take long to come round. And when the squad told him all about Jimbo's deadline, he perked *right* up.

He'd never been a big fan of Princey's. And now if he could find someone to buy the club, he could make a nice little commission for himself too. For some people, money talks. For Neil Veal it sang – very, very loudly.

But luckily he loved plastic too. He had fistfuls of credit cards with him, so he took the players to a hole in the wall and dished out an awful lot of Italian hard currency to tide them over. "Wow!" breathed Chrissie, holding up one of the notes. "Twenty-five thousand lire! How much is *that* worth in proper money?"

"About twenty quid," Cool F told him. "And it won't go far here."

"Hey now," said Vealy, when everyone had their dosh. "I'll need time and space to go through my little black book. I've gotta find us all a new hotel too. So why don't you go get an eyeful of the sights – then meet me back here at four?"

"Good call!" said Craig. "I want to have a go in one of those gondolas!"

"That's in *Verona*, dummy," Keats told him. "Or is it Venice?"

"Well I'm heading for an ice-cream parlour," Madman declared, licking his lips and rubbing his already tubby tummy.

"Don't go pigging out," Dennis warned him. "We've got a game tomorrow."

"No worries," Madman grinned. "Just one Cornetto!"

"Whatever you do," said Gaffer, shaking his head, "just make sure you stay in pairs. We don't want anyone getting lost. I'll stay with you, Dog, OK?"

Dog looked at him with great seriousness. He still had his helmet on from the long ride and he was covered in dust, yet he looked as fresh as a daisy. "I am," he said in a voice so deep that it rumbled, "exceedingly pleased to meet you."

Luke teamed up with Fred and set off on a quest to find the ruins of the Colosseum. Luke had been amazed when their History teacher had told them all about it. Apparently, on combat days, the ancient Roman spectators took a big part in the action. When a gladiator was defeated, it was up to the crowd whether he lived or died. A wave of a hanky and he was spared. A turned-down thumb and off he went for an early bath in the next world. Good job they didn't give the same power to Division Three football crowds.

But at first the boys got nowhere near the Colosseum. Cool F had a pretty good sense of what direction to go in, but they were out in broad daylight in one of the most football-mad cities in the world. At almost every street corner somebody would catch a glimpse of them, whistle and wave to all their mates, then mob them with desperate requests for autographs.

"Studless Senzatione!!!" they would cry. "Coolius Caesar!!!" It was pretty clear that the locals were all rooting for the English under-dogs in the upcoming Final. "You will murder Barcelona by four goals to nil!" yelled one very large man in a chef's hat who dashed out of his restaurant to give them both complimentary Quattro Stagioni pizzas. "But not, alas, if *Il Principe* plays."

"Well," said Luke as he autographed his apron while listening to the TAFKAG album blasting away inside, "we're working on that."

They kept to backstreets afterwards, and got a bit lost. Then as soon as they hit another main road, they were dragged into a Gucci shop and made to sign the soles of pretty well every pair of shoes in the window. They got some smart loafers in return though – little leather miracles that would probably have cost several million lire if they'd been paying.

After that Luke and Frederick looked at each other, nodded, then found a shop to buy coats with collars they could turn up, hats with brims they could turn down and – a nice final touch – a couple of red women's wigs. (TAFKAG's peculiar racket was flooding that shop too. He really was *big* news over here. Had anyone since the Beatles ever shot to international mega-stardom quite so fast?)

At last the boys now got a bit of peace and quiet. In their disguises they sweltered under the hot Mediterranean sun, but after crossing the river they got their bearings again – and nearly made it as far as the Colosseum.

Nearly, but not quite. In a wide open space full of old ruins – the Roman Forum according to Frederick – both boys were electrified by a strangled female screech:

"Lu-u-u-u-u-u-u-ke!!!!!"

When you hear a noise like that, you don't hang around waiting to find out who's made it. Luke and Frederick knew all about the nuttier kind of fan. The sort that wants a bit of your leg or ear to take home and treasure as a souvenir. The only thing to do in these cases is run, fast, as far from it as possible.

But as they raced off towards the House of the Vestal Virgins, the awesome racket came at them again. And this time it sounded closer:

"Lu-u-u-u-u-u-ke! COME BACK!..."

Luke and Fred swapped glances. Pretty good English for a madwoman. But in taking his eyes off where he was running, Luke didn't see a small dog wander out on to the path and stand smack-bang in his way. It was just the kind of thing Jimbo did when an opposing forward was bearing down on the Albion goal.

Luke didn't exactly tread on the doggie. As his foot came down, it scuttled away with a split-second to spare. But Luke felt the breeze, tilted sideways, collided with Cool F, and they both toppled down on the grass verge.

"Lu-u-u-u-u-u-u-ke!" came the scream again. Louder than ever, and this time there as no getting away. Luke and Frederick scrambled to their feet but the owner of that awesome voice was now looming above them – hands on hips, blazing-eyed, mouth twisted in fury, Albion bobble-hat askew.

"Mum!" gasped Luke.

"What *do* you think you're doing!" she panted. "Dressed up like a moron and running away from me? Didn't you *hear* me calling? I've a good mind to give you a good hiding right here and now..."

"Er – sorry, Mum," said Luke, putting his wig straight and pulling his hat down again. "Oh, hi there, Rodney."

"Hello, boys," puffed Luke's stepdad, catching up with his wife. "What a coincidence seeing you two here! Your mum just wanted to take a look at these marvellous trees. Is – um – everything all right?"

Luke looked at Fred. "Well," he admitted, "not really..." And together they filled them in on the players' strike – and on Jimbo's strike back.

19

Luke's mum threw an awesome open-air wobbler when she heard the full story. Luckily the four of them were already standing in a place full of ruins. Otherwise she might have demolished that old Roman Forum single-handed.

In the end Rodney got her sorted. He took her for a few turns among the orange trees, oleanders and cypresses, which calmed her down a bit. She would have died for a garden that looked like that. (Even so, she muttered, a few well-chosen garden gnomes would have made a *big* improvement.)

"Anyway, Mum," said Luke, "Fred and I are running a bit late now. We were meant to be meeting Vealy and the rest at four o'clock…"

"Anywhere that you go now, we go too," she told him flat. "I don't trust that Neil Veal as far as I could kick him. I want to see *exactly* what sort of a hotel he's found for you."

And that was that. There was no point in Luke or Fred protesting. She'd made up her mind. So back they all went to the cashpoint over the river, where they expected to find most of the rest of the squad already waiting. But only Chrissie was there – kitted out in a Rastafarian wig, false nose and glasses. Obviously he'd had the same trouble as Luke and Fred with mobs of Italian fans. "I'm roasting under this lot," he sighed. "I never knew Italy was so hot." Then his eyes popped. "Oh, hello Mrs Green. What are you doing here?"

"Never you mind about me," she snorted, looking all round at the multitudes of tourists. "Where in heaven's name is everyone else?"

"Oh, Vealy took them all off to this hotel he's found. Over by the main train station. Cheap but cheerful, he said it was. He left me here with the address, to show Luke and Fred the way. So come on then, boys, let's get a move on. Look, Vealy gave me some dosh for a taxi." He waved a handful of notes as a yellow cab passed by and its driver slammed on the brakes to pull up.

But as soon as Chrissie jumped inside, he turned to find Luke's mum and Rodney following him in – as well as his two team-mates.

"I don't like the sound of this hotel," Mrs G declared. "Places near stations are never very pleasant. All that soot and smoke." Rod rolled his eyes at Luke; she clearly thought they still had steam trains in Italy. "If I don't like the look of it, I'm taking Luke back to the guest-house that Rodney and I are staying in. Although even *that*'s not what I would call spotlessly clean, despite the fact that we're paying an absolute *fortune* to be staying there…"

She went on like this for most of the taxi-ride back into the city centre. Luke had long ago learned how to keep nodding while paying no attention whatsoever. His own thoughts were full of Neil Veal. Had Vealo possibly had any luck in finding a buyer for Albion? He had seemed pretty confident. But Luke wasn't so sure. It was *such* short notice. And Jimbo had paid £7 million for Albion the year before – so, knowing him, he would probably want about £10 million for it now…

His heart sank as the taxi-driver turned down a dark and narrow sidestreet next to the huge station. Sleazy? Some soot and smoke might have smartened it *up*.

Raggedy kids were climbing all over the parked cars. Drunks clutching bottles of wine were propped up asleep in almost every doorway. And – worst of all – a really evil bunch of guys was blocking off the end of the road: gangster hats with wide brims, outsized suits, wraparound shades. Either they were holding a *Godfather* lookalike competition in the grotty building behind them, or else they were about to tear apart the taxi with their bare hands.

The driver drew to a halt. Luke gulped, but then he looked again. The gang of Godfathers looked so menacing. But there behind them was a more reassuring sight. A pantomime lion in a blue-and-white-hooped shirt. It was Kingsley Castle, the Albion mascot! Then glancing back at the nearest Godfathers he saw that one was carrying a pineapple, another an ice-cream cone. And suddenly he recognized Carl, Craig, Dog, Madman, Casper and Keatsy. It was just another set of disguises. Whooping with relief, Luke reached out to open the door and get out. He never got as far as the handle.

"You stay where you are!" his mum barked. "If that's the hotel you're meant to be staying in, you can forget it." She nodded at the frontage. Several of the windows were broken. *Kit-e-Kat*, it said in big pink letters. (Luke had to be honest: a hotel named after a brand of cat-food *didn't* look promising.) "That's no place for a young boy. You'd probably have your throat slit in the night."

"But Mum," protested Luke as Chrissie escaped to join the Godfathers, followed by Cool F, "I've got to be with the rest of the squad. I don't even know what's happening about Jimbo and the club yet."

"Then ask – quickly." Luke's mum wound down the window and beckoned to Godfather One – Craig – to come over. At once he obeyed.

Luke shrugged helplessly up at him. "How's it going, Craig?" he said. "Has Vealy had any luck? Have we got a buyer?"

"Nice outfits, eh?" he grinned, plucking at his suit jacket. "But oh wow, what an afternoon! Vealy's made so many calls, the battery's gone dead on his mobile. He's using the phone inside the hotel now. It's been difficult. Especially since he got through to Jimbo. Wait for this. Our beloved chairman says he wants £20 million for the club and he won't take a penny less."

"*Twenty!*" gasped everyone in the car, including the taxi-driver.

"Yeah. So Vealy's pulling out all the stops. Trying all his showbiz contacts. All the Spice Girls, Richard Branson, Kate Winslet, Chris Evans ... even Chris Tarrant. (He asked if he could phone a friend then never rang back.) Then there were those blokes in Oasis. They were *quite* interested – but only if we changed our name to 'Manchester City Two' and agreed to play in an emptied-out swimming pool, on motorbikes. I think they were winding him up, actually..."

"Look!" Luke's mum interrupted him. She'd had more than enough of this, and she was itching to get out of that dismal street. "What you're saying is that you haven't found anyone?"

"As things stand – well, no. We haven't."

"And you've got till midday tomorrow to buy the club from that rotten little nitwit?"

"That's right. He's already fixed up a noon press conference – at that hotel he kicked us out of. Either we take someone there to stump up the cash, or he'll pull all his money out of Albion and just kill off the club."

"Right," said Luke's mum, starting to wind the window back up. She had a grim, determined look in her eye. The sort she had when she was trying hard to remember where she'd hidden the cooking sherry in the kitchen. "I'll see what I can do."

"*You?*" cried Luke, Rod and Craig.

"Me!" she cried back. "Somebody's got to sort out this ridiculous mess – and it's obviously not going to be any of you lot!" She reached forward and tapped the driver on the shoulder – pretty hard. "Now get me out of this dump!"

20

If Luke got a wink of sleep that night, he didn't remember it.

He was *way* too wound up wondering what the next day might bring. His mum hadn't let him ring the squad's hotel. (What did she think? That he might get his throat slit over the phone?) But she'd been making lots of calls herself, shut away in the bedroom. Sometimes Rod and Luke heard her yelling, but they couldn't for the life of them work out who she was giving such a hard time to.

"I mean," whispered Rodney, shaking his head at Luke, "who does *she* know who might be able to save the club? The only person she talks to on a regular basis are the people at the Garden Centre. Oh, and your Auntie Evelyn – and she can't even afford to get her portable TV fixed."

Luke screwed up his face, baffled. There was just one possibility, he thought. It seemed a bit far-fetched – and he didn't want to mention it to

Rodney, just in case he got jealous. It all went back to that night in France after the semi-final victory over Paris St Germain. The night of Luke's mum's miraculous conversion to football. No one quite knew how Des Lynam had won her over. But maybe they had stayed in touch, and now she was trying to get Des to help out in the club's darkest hour.

Finally, long after dawn, Luke managed to doze off. In a way he wished he hadn't. He had one horrible dream after another. In one of them Jimbo was buzzing about over Ash Acre in his private jet and dropping exploding pineapple-bombs on the Pants Protesters. In another, all the reporters at the noon press conference were laughing as Luke's mum stood up and started counting £1 coins out of her purse in a bid to buy the club herself. In yet another, Benny Webb had been sent into a jam-packed Colosseum, still wearing his sheepskin, to fight bare-handed with a pack of snarling wolves...

"No, no, no!" Luke came awake shouting. "Not the wolves!!!"

"No, lad," said someone with a very deep voice, putting a calming hand on his shoulder. "Not Wolves, it's Barcelona. Here, today. The game of your life!"

"Grandpa!" Luke cried, blinking the sleep out of his eyes. "And Nan!"

"Hello, my love," said Nan at his camp-bedside.

"We dropped in from our own hotel to say hello to Rodney and your mum. We had no *idea* we'd find you here too. Ooh, it's a bit naughty what Jimbo's doing, isn't it? Holding the club to ransom like this. He needs a good smack on the bottom."

"Aye, well," said Grandpa, "that's as may be. I'll be glad enough to see the back of him – as long as we can find someone to give him his twenty million."

"Which doesn't look too likely, I'm afraid," said Rodney from the chair in the corner. "I've been ringing Gaffer and the squad all morning. They haven't had any joy. Twenty million pounds is an awful lot of money."

"Well, it is and it isn't," Nan sighed. "You couldn't even buy David Beckham's right-hand side for that much nowadays, could you? It's all wrong, isn't it?"

"Anyway, Luke," said Rod, standing, "we've let you sleep in – just in *case* you've got a game today. But it's past eleven o'clock now. So you'd better get dressed and we'll whizz over to this press conference. You never know – Jimbo might have had second thoughts and decided not to be such a silly boy."

The other three stared at him in disbelief. Rod always tried to look on the bright side of things, but this was just plain crazy. Jimbo – not be silly? As if!

"Hold on, though," said Luke when he'd pulled on his jeans. "Where's Mum?"

"Search me," said Rod. "She's been out since eight this morning. I'm sure she *thinks* she knows what she's doing." But even Brightside Rodney didn't sound too convinced by this. And Grandpa and Nan just snorted. As far as they were concerned, their grown-up daughter *still* needed regular smacks on the bottom.

After a quick bite of breakfast, the four of them took a taxi and headed in brilliant sunshine up to the Hotel Garibaldi. Luke had forgotten to put on his disguise so he nearly got pulled to pieces by the huge crowd outside it. Most of them were blue-and-white-clad Albion fans, and they all looked frantic.

"What's going on, Luke?" one hollered. "What's this press conference about?" bellowed another. "Is it serious?" "Is Jimbo gonna bring Benny back?" "*What's going on?*"

All Luke could do was shake his head and fight his way through into the foyer. It amazed him that they still didn't know what had gone off. Even Rocky Mitford, right at the front, looked completely bewildered.

"Where have you players *been*, Luke?" he asked. "Why haven't you been staying here? What's Jimbo going to announce? *What's happening to our club?*"

Luke glanced at his watch. It was three

minutes to twelve. "I can't talk now, Rocky," he said, then he grabbed him by his huge arm. "Come on in with us. Find out for yourself." And none of the guards tried to stop him.

Rodney, Nan, Grandpa, Luke and Rocky dashed through to the vast ground-floor conference room. So many reporters had turned up that some had to watch and listen from outside in the corridor. At first it looked as if Luke's group would have to do the same. But Grandpa wasn't having any of that. He lifted one scribbling hack right out of the way, then the rest cleared a path.

There were no chairs. Everyone was standing shoulder-to-shoulder, sardine-tight, just like on the terraces back at good old Ash Acre. At once Luke saw the backs of several heads he knew: Gaffer, Carl, Kingsley Castle (what was *he* doing in here?). There was Narris, and Half-Fat. And that was Keatsy over there with Darius. But not – as far as Luke could see – any Veal.

Up on a raised stage, there was a table bristling with microphones. Six of Jimbo's security men sat behind them, all stone silent. In the middle was Jimbo, only an inch or so taller, even though he was standing. He was wearing a nerdy businessman's suit and tie, not his miniature sheepskin. And he was halfway through reading a short speech from a scrap of paper: "...so since the players have refused to play in tonight's game, I have no option but to pull Castle Albion out of the UEFA Cup, giving Barcelona a walkover victory..." The crystal chandeliers all tinkled from the enormous gasp of amazement that swept through the room. "And since I regard this as unacceptable behaviour on the part of the players, I have decided to withdraw all my support from Castle Albion FC. The club will now cease to exist..."

"*Oh no it won't!*" screeched a female voice above the frenzy of noise that went up at this news. For a dizzying moment, Luke couldn't trace the voice. Then he heard it again: "You said the club had till noon to find a new owner, you little twit, and there's still a minute to go!" And then Luke saw.

Clambering up on to the stage from a door at the back was ... his mum! On her own. Albion bobble-hat on her head, blue-and-white klaxon horn in one hand. What was she ranting on about? Had she finally flipped altogether?

Two of the security guys shot to their feet and took a step towards her. But even they paused then, and glanced at Jimbo for instructions. He blinked and waved her forward, up to the microphones which she hardly needed.

She stalked forward, stooped towards the nearest mike but didn't sit. "I don't know what he's been telling you," she announced, turning to clip the back of Jimbo's head. "But none of this is the players' fault. *He*'s caused all the trouble from start to finish." Now she grabbed his ear and tweaked it. "He can't play and he can't manage. And the players just told him that. So he told *them* to find someone to give him £20 million for the club or else he would close it down..."

More chandelier-shaking greeted this revelation. And Luke noticed a grinning Neil Veal sliding on to the stage though the back door, holding a sheaf of papers. And there was someone else behind him in the doorway. Who was this shadowy someone? Des Lynam? Maybe. Luke couldn't be sure.

"Well, Mr Prat of a Prince," Luke's mum roared on, "a saviour has now been found!" Veal nodded. Jimbo frowned, then ducked in case she molested him again. "He's a bit of a twit himself, so he took a lot of persuading from me and his idiotic agent here. And we had to negotiate long and hard this morning with his record company to get all the cash up front. But it now gives me the greatest pleasure to introduce to you the next chairman of Castle Albion FC..."

She beckoned to the back doorway and in came ... a huge cardboard cheque – blocking from view the guy carrying it, except for his feet. The cheque was made out to Jimbo for £20 million, and everyone in the room tried like mad to decipher the signature at the bottom. Luke, however, didn't need to do that. He had already recognized those thirty-year-old snakeskin boots.

Then his mum took one end of the cheque, Vealy took the other, and as they lowered it every single person in the room including Jimbo now suddenly cried out in astonishment: "TAFKAG!"

21

It took a good five minutes to restore order in the room. Outside of a football ground, Luke had never heard such an uproar. Pants flew, players cheered in totally unexpected glee. Somehow the news got outside too – and the noise the Albion faithful made nearly lifted the building off its foundations.

But the person who looked most flabber-gasted of all was TAFKAG himself. And it was easy to see why. *Twenty million pounds!* It was a good job they hadn't written out that figure on the cheque in Italian lire. There would never have been enough room for all the noughts. Twenty *million*!

Until his recent rise to fame, Luke's dad had been sleeping in his van most nights. He hadn't bought any new clothes since the end of the Sixties (although that was partly through personal choice). He hadn't even had a bank account until last year. And now he was shelling out a cool twenty million quid for a run-down club that had just finished 91st out of 92 in the League! Kooky!

Luke later found out that most of this money wasn't even his. Dosh was pouring in from his global album sales, and *one day* he might own twenty mill. But in the meantime – mainly thanks to an Oscar-winning display of bullying from Luke's mum – his record company was making him a massive loan. He might well end up paying it back for the rest of his life. So no wonder he now looked as if he'd been coshed over the head. In fact, in "persuading" him to save the Albion, Luke's mum might even have done that too.

But the main point was that Albion *had* been saved. As hundreds of cameras flashed and hundreds of newsmen and women tried in vain to make themselves heard, Jimbo went silently over to TAFKAG and shook his hand. The deal was done. Jimbo was out, TAFKAG was in. Nightmare over, now dream on! And just before his security staff could close in around him, Luke's mum couldn't resist a parting shot: a blast from her Albion klaxon horn, right in his ear.

Jimbo twisted round and glared at her through his glasses. But before he could say a word, Madman hurled something soft, grey and Y-fronted at him from down on the floor. It was a perfect shot. The keeper's single, historic pair of pants wrapped themselves around Jimbo's face, shutting him up for good.

At that point Vealy intervened, removed the offending undergarment and suggested that Princey should accompany him backstage to sign all the necessary papers. Which, thankfully, the ex-player-chairman-manager did, followed by his little private army who carried off the great cardboard cheque. And that left just Luke's mum and dad on the stage.

TAFKAG looked at her, she pointed impatiently at the microphones, and up he went to sit at the table.

"Er ... hey there!" he grinned, blinking out into the blitz of flashing cameras. He raised two fingers in a peace sign, then fiddled with his ponytail. "Groovy, yeah? I've always really – um – dug the Albion, and I'll – ah – get a major buzz now out of being the main man. So – er – well, I think that's about it really…"

"Oh for heaven's *sake*!" yelled Luke's mum, coming up and sitting next to him. "Do I have to do *everything* around here?! How about appointing a new manager? That's what this has all been *about*, hasn't it, you ditzy old hippie?!"

"R-i-i-i-ght," drawled TAFKAG, nodding, and inching away from her just in case she biffed him one for good measure too. (It must have been just like the old days for him, Luke thought.) But where *was* the only possible manager? Luke wasn't the only person scanning the room for a glimpse of Big Benny.

Then TAFKAG beckoned to a figure on the floor. Everyone caught their breath as Kingsley Castle began to head for the stage. "Wick-*ed*!" breathed Cool F, who had found his way to Luke's side in the crowd.

"There's only one cat who deserves the name of 'Boss' at Castle Albion," TAFKAG went on, getting to his feet to give Kingsley a hand up. "He's come in disguise to keep all you news-hounds and *paparazzi* off his trail," he yelled as the Albion mascot started tugging his own head off. "Now you've all heard of Fantastic Mr Fox! It gives me the biggest kick on earth to welcome back: Wonderful Mr Webb!"

And there at last he was: Benny! His ruffled-up hair and beard poking out of the great fawn body of Kingsley Castle – and even inside that little furnace he still had his sheepskin coat on! Was this a proper manager, or what?

To an avalanche of applause, Benny tried to look as solemn as anyone could in half a lion's body. He nodded, closed his eyes, then raised one hand for silence.

"Friends, Romans, countrymen," he began. "This is a big day for me, and let's hope it's gonna be an even bigger one for Castle Albion. At the end of the day, this game is all about the fans. Ordinary everyday blokes and ladies and kiddies – not billionaire businessmen. A true fan has bought this club today. Thousands of other fans are in this city now, waiting to see a Third Division side win everlastin' European glory. That's their dream. That's my players' dream. It's my dream too. And dreams, you know, really can come true…"

As fresh applause broke out, Luke's mum surged to her feet and grabbed a microphone. "OK then!" she screamed, swept up in the torrent of emotion but with real menace in her voice. "That's enough hot air! The Boss needs to get back together with his players now. They've got a date with destiny here tonight in Rome's Olympic Stadium. So let's just wish them all the best as they take on Spain's Real Madrid to win the European Champions' League!!!"

Briefly everyone paused and frowned, then they all just clapped anyway. With her in that sort of mood, it was a whole lot safer than trying to put her straight.

22

It was as if he'd never been away. Benny took the squad – plus Terry, Ruel and Mrs Bowman – straight to the Olympic Stadium and put them through their first proper workout since the Northampton game.

If the Boss was emotional about his return, he kept it well hidden. Most of the time he was effing and blinding at one player or another. "What have you been doin' since I got the bullet?!" he kept ranting. "You look as if you've never even *seen* a football, half of you!" But the only player he actually hit was Carl.

"Tell me, Boss," gasped a breathless Mr Pineapple Pants during a break between exercises, "are away goals gonna count double tonight or not?"

"Are you nuts?" Benny spat back. "Who's the away team then?"

Carl looked baffled. "Well – us. Barcelona are Italian, aren't they?"

Benny didn't bother to answer that. He just

took a swipe at Carl's wavy-haired head and rolled his eyes in despair. (Carl looked quite pleased really; at last he could forget all about maths and concentrate on football. The rest looked pretty pleased too. It was so great to be getting back to normal.) But as the Boss pointed out after a short, sharp and highly skilful practice match, Barcelona weren't exactly Spanish nowadays either. "Van Gaal the coach is Dutch," Benny explained, "and half his team come from Holland too: Hesp the keeper, Bogarde at the back, the de Boer brothers, Kluivert the silky striker…"

"Then you've got the Portuguese guy up front on the right," Terry went on.

"Fido," Chrissie added helpfully, glancing at Dog.

"Figo!" Ruel corrected him. "And we mustn't forget a certain Brazilian ex-World Footballer of the Year…"

"How could we," grinned Narris. "Rivaldo, eh? But he's only got one decent foot, hasn't he?"

"Trouble is," nodded Dennis the Novelist, "it's more like a magic wand."

Terry clapped his hands as everyone started looking a bit awestruck. "Come on now, lads! Just think about it: we're putting the wind right up them too. Even as we speak, Rivaldo will be muttering to Guardiola: 'That Craig Edwards, we'll have to watch him coming forward. And as for Half-Fat Milkes, he's *wicked*!'"

"I can just hear it," grunted Benny, glancing down at a few scribbled notes he'd made during the days of his exile. "Right then, lads – one last thing before you go back indoors. Penalties."

"That's OK Boss," said Craig. "If we give any away, Madman will save 'em. He always does. It's just about the only thing he *can* do."

"That's as maybe," Benny replied. "But I'm not talking about giving the things away in open play. I'm more concerned that we'll be deadlocked after extra-time, and then the whole business will be decided by a penalty shoot-out."

"Yeah," shrugged Casper. "But Madman will still save them all, won't he?"

Benny glared at him. "But we've still got to score ours, *haven't* we? And when did you lot last have a practice from twelve yards? We've gotta do this, lads. I keep remembering the European Cup Final of 1986. Barcelona were in that one too – managed by a certain Terry Venables. It went to pens and Barcelona missed the lot. Never seen anything like it. That's not gonna happen to us!"

Then he sent Madman in for an early bath. "It'll only demoralize this lot if you keep saving their best shots," he explained. Then he put

Gaffer in between the sticks and invited each player in turn to "pot the white".

"Pot the white?" laughed Keatsy as Darius stepped up first. "He couldn't pot a plant." And indeed, he blazed his shot way over. A quite horrendous display of miskicks, wide slices and woodwork-thumping followed, with only Luke and Cool F tucking the ball away, and even Cool F's went in off a post.

Benny had been right. This aspect of Albion's game was in need of a lot of work – and that's what it got. Over an hour later, Gaffer was being beaten every single time – thanks to a stream of useful tips from the Big Boss. No one now had an excuse for missing, if and when the shoot-out moment came.

After everyone had washed and changed, and taken a light late lunch, Benny let the players speak to the world's media for an hour or so. ("Do you think you've got a prayer of winning?" one French journalist asked Narris. "Well everyone's got a prayer," Phizzo replied. "Barça have got more than you, though," the journalist smiled back. "The Pope is one of their supporters.") Then Benny hauled them all back into the depths of the Olympic Stadium. Already the seats outside were starting to fill up, as kick-off time approached fast. The atmosphere in the fabulous ground was building, building, building...

"I want you all to take a look at this," said Ben, slipping a video into a slot under a wall-wide screen. "Everyone keeps saying Barcelona are the world's biggest club, the world's best team by a mile, all that guff. Well, I want you to forget all about Spain and Italy and basically *anywhere* foreign now. You lot all play in the world's toughest League. I want you to be proud of that. Proud of the strengths and traditions of English football. At our best, when we really get stuck in, we're a match for anyone on this planet. There's no answer to the British bulldog spirit! Just sit back and remind yourselves of that now..."

The room darkened. What followed on the screen needed *at least* a PG certificate. So this was what Benny did in his spare time. It was a compilation tape he'd made of lower-division highlights – a lot of it so old that it was in grainy black and white. No Manchester Uniteds or Liverpools here. Just Bournemouths and Brentfords and Darlingtons and Notts Counties. All honest, no-frills professional footballers, doing what English League footballers did best – getting stuck in, showing the odd bit of skill, but basically giving two hundred per cent as they tore around the pitch sweating blood for the cause of their teams. One for all and all for one. Battling as if their very lives depended on it.

When it was over, Luke felt exhausted. He

could almost feel the bruises too. But in an odd way, it *had* been inspiring. Benny was right. Players like Dennis and Gaffer and Chrissie could never hope to match the Boys in Barcelona's Blue and Red for technique. But they *could* shake them up a bit. They could give them a UEFA-Cup-Final-sized dose of what had always made the English game great.

"Go and get changed now, lads," Benny said before shaking each player firmly by the hand. "There are games to see and there are games not to miss. There are games to play in and games to win. I really fancy your chances here tonight." He twitched his nose. "And I smell goals. Goals that will bring this cup home to Albion! I've said and done all I can. Now it's over to you. Go get 'em, eh?"

23

For Luke – and probably everyone else connected with Albion – it was the ultimate "pinch-me-I'm-dreaming" moment.

Standing on the pitch with a minute to go to kick-off, he gazed around the massive stadium, packed with 80,000 baying spectators. With all due respect to the Nationwide League, this certainly was a notch up from Northampton.

And it was light years away from crumbling old Ash Acre, which was now, of course, the club's home once again. You could have filled Ash Acre three times over with just the blue-and-white-hooped hordes who were now ready and waiting in here. And if Luke's life had taken a different turn, two years before, he would have been in among them: all done up in a replica kit, beside himself with excitement before watching the biggest game of his life.

But to have got into the Albion *team* – that was his first dream come true. To have won the FA Cup with them – that was the second. And now, *now* – he stood on this Olympic turf, right on the verge of immortal European glory...

"Pinch me," he said in amazement to Cool F. "Pinch me hard."

But his best mate just nodded and touched fists with him. "Big yourself up," he said. "There's no way we're gonna walk away from here without winning."

Luke looked into his eyes. He clearly wasn't talking about Gaffer winning the toss against Barça skipper Figo – which he'd just done. This was the time to stand up and be counted (as long as Carl Davey wasn't doing the counting). Luke nodded back. They had taken such a long and winding road to get here. Having arrived at last, why not win? That would be the *real* icing on the jelly.

He took a last look around. Everything was in place. Benny, Terry and Ruel in the dug-out. His own dad in the chairman's seat. His mum, Rodney, Nan and Grandpa up in the VIP boxes. Rocky Mitford and the Best Fans in Britain (minus a few pairs of pants now) poised in their seats to jump for joy at the first Albion strike of the night. All that remained was to win the thing...

The Belgian ref blew his whistle and off they went. Or rather, off Barça went. They hadn't won their reputation as the world's best attacking side for nothing. And they seemed to want to make that clear right away. For the best part of a quarter of an hour, the ball hardly left the Albion half. Prompted by wide runs from the back by Bogarde and Puyol, midfielders Cocu and Gabri took the game by the scruff of the neck, and fed a succession of short, amazingly accurate passes to the awesome Barça front three: Rivaldo, Kluivert and Figo.

The ball moved around at a supernatural speed. If it had been a player, it would have been given an immediate drugs test. But the Barça boys seemed to have no trouble controlling it, even when they themselves were moving like trains. Gaffer and his defence had to dig deep to keep them at bay. And to be fair, they didn't do a bad job.

For all Barcelona's possession, and all the noise that came from their rabid fans, they managed only two serious strikes on Madman's goal. The first was a wicked dipping volley from Frank de Boer which the keeper lost sight of in the air, but which dropped just wide of his left-hand post. Then, after a crisp interchange of passes, Guardiola put Kluivert clean through on goal.

The tall, lean Dutchman, cutting in from the right, left Gaffer for dead and found himself one-on-one with Madman. Luke – too far away to have any effect at all – went up on the toes of his trainers in terror. Kluivert let Madman dash out to narrow the angle, then dinked a lovely little chip around him. It looked like 1-0 all the way – till it struck the near post and rolled across the face of goal. Madman was stranded, but Kluivert followed up like lightning.

Unluckily for him, lightning wasn't quite fast enough. Cool F spotted the danger in advance, hared back, slid in and scooped the ball far away to safety upfield.

"One Frederick Dulac!"
rose up in relief from the Albion ranks.

**"There's Only One Frederick Dulac!!
One Freddie DU-LA-AC!!! And He Plays At The
BACK!"**

It wasn't the most original rhyme that Rocky's lot had ever dreamed up on the spur of the moment. But they were worried fans up there – and with good reason. Just when it seemed that the Barça onslaught must cease for a while, and so let Albion start getting a kick, they seemed to find yet another gear. Once again they came forward in their fast-passing waves – twice more hitting the woodwork before the half-hour mark.

Luke couldn't remember a game when he himself had been less involved. It wasn't just that Barça had so much possession. For whenever he, Chrissie, Half-Fat or Narris managed to get their foot on it, they were swamped at once by their opposite numbers desperate to get it back. At times it seemed as if Albion were playing against twenty-two men, not just eleven.

But in football you get no points for possession or artistic effect. Goals are what matters, and as the game began to race towards half-time, the scoresheet stayed blank – which had to be good news for the Albion. *Surely*, thought Luke, Barça couldn't keep up this sort of pressure for the full ninety minutes. There would have to be a let-up sometime, and that might just give the underdogs their chance.

As if to prove his point, in the forty-third minute Albion suddenly got a break. Bogarde had powered forward yet again along the left flank. Outpacing Narris, he then tried to beat Half-Fat who had dashed across to cover. But he pushed the ball just too far past him, Cool F nicked it away, then laid it straight up to Luke. For once the Studless Sensation didn't have two Barça battlers breathing down his back. At least six of their players were stranded deep in the Albion half, into which they had rushed forward with Bogarde.

Luke looked ahead of him. Hesp in the Barcelona goal was a distant figure. But directly in between there were only three players: Abelardo and Puyol for the opposition, and a certain Dogan Mezir in blue-and-white hoops. Luke didn't think twice. Nor did the Dog. Like a terrier seeing his master shaping up to hurl a stick for him to chase, as soon as the thunder-thighed striker saw Luke taking aim, he shot between the two defenders – and got on the end of his inch-perfect through ball before either of them could turn.

That was stunning enough. Then came the knock-out blow. Dog was thirty yards out when the ball dropped in front of him. Hesp was on the edge of his six-yard box. Expecting Dog to advance on him as Kluivert had done on Madman earlier, he shuffled and spread himself, trying to get all his angles right. He needn't have bothered. Dog didn't even wait for the ball to hit the deck. Instead he *side-footed* it from all of thirty yards, high and handsome over the clutching hands of Hesp and into the far corner of his net.

One-nil to the Albion! THIS was what they meant by the bulldog spirit!

"Woof-Woof! Woof! Woof! Woof-Woof! WOOF!"

The hooped half of the stadium erupted in chaotic celebration. Rome had never seen so many inflatable tandems hurled skywards, not to mention all the Carl-Davey-style inflatable pineapples that went up after them. Meanwhile the Dog himself disappeared under every single one of his joyous team-mates.

Which meant that none of them saw the ref's assistant flagging for all he was worth over by the dug-out touchline. But the ref saw. Across he raced, and in a flash Benny, Ruel and Tel were rocketing assistant-wards too. No – surely *not*! Bamboozled by the Dog's sheer speed, the man with the flag believed that he must have been in an offside position when Luke had hit the pass!

Firmly, repeatedly, he shook his head at the ref to indicate no goal. And however much Rocky and Co, *then* Benny and Co, *then* Gaffer and Co all screamed that he was off his head, the ref paid no heed and gave a goal-kick.

Dog just couldn't believe it. As Hesp set the ball down for the kick, the shaggy-haired Armenian followed the ref right back to the half-way line, waving his arms and yelling in his own language.

"*What* did you say?" the ref finally yelled back in perfect English, turning round to face him.

Dog flung out his arms in despair. As a last resort he glared at the man in black and boomed at him: "*I am exceedingly pleased to meet you!*"

And the ref immediately reached for a yellow card and flourished it over his head. He hadn't understood all the protests in Armenian. But he knew when a player was taking the micky out of him in English. Into the book went Dog.

There was hardly time left for Barça to mount

another attack before the half-time whistle. Off trooped the Albion lads, still fuming that they had been robbed. But they all knew there was a long, long way to go yet.

By special arrangement with the stadium officials, Mrs Bowman brought the squad its half-time tea. Benny didn't pick up the tray of mugs and hurl the whole lot at the wall, but he might just as well have done. For fifteen minutes the Sheepskin Supremo gave a match-day masterclass in lid-flipping.

"Apart for that last move, you just weren't at the races!" he stormed. "You look sluggish! You look scared! You don't look *smart* – and if there's one thing I can't stand it's stupid footballers!" The players stared down at their boots (or in Luke's case, his trainers) and waited for the thunder and lightning to pass. With Benny – unlike Jimbo – it always did. He just had to get it all out of his system. So in the end, with all the tea drunk, a humming silence fell.

"You've got to be fair, though," piped up Craig. "We've had the ball in the net and they haven't. *And* it was a goal, whichever way you look at it."

"Not if you're the flippin' ref's assistant, it wasn't," muttered Benny. "You've got to put that diabolical injustice behind you now. There's only one way we're going to go home with this Cup, and that's by working our socks off for the next forty-five minutes..."

"And all through extra time too, if needs be," added Terry.

"Or until somebody gets a Golden Goal," Ruel pointed out, because if the game went into extra time, the first goal scored by either side would win it.

"Yeah, yeah, yeah," Benny shouted over them, clenching both fists. "Now get yourselves out there again and show those Spanish bullfighters that *this* British bulldog's still got a whole lot of life left in him!"

The squad looked baffled for a moment, picturing a matador twirling his red cloak above a grunting old pooch. Then up the players jumped and with a mass bark they charged out to resume battle with the brilliant Barcelonans.

But though they now huffed and puffed enough to satisfy even Benny's sky-high standards of huffery and puffery, it didn't make very much difference. During the interval Louis van Gaal had obviously told Barça to up *their* effort as well. Gone were the magical moves of the first forty-five. Now they took a far more physical approach, trying to bulldoze their way past Albion's defenders rather than bamboozle them with beautiful football.

So, with Barça bulldozing and Albion bull-dogging, the second half turned out to be less about soccer than slugging-it-out. All over the park bone-crunching tackles went in, every fifty-fifty ball was contested as if the future of the planet depended on it, and both on the field and off it temperatures started to soar. It didn't get dirty, exactly. Only one more player on either side – Barcelona's Gabri – was cautioned. But as the game entered its last quarter, all the muscular challenges had taken a heavy toll.

Figo and Cocu both limped off, to be replaced by Litmanen and Luis Enrique. Half-Fat took no further part after running into Abelardo, and he gave way to Darius. Then Dennis came off second-best in an aerial duel with Rivaldo, hit the deck awkwardly, and had to be trolleyed into touch. Casper came on for him, but slotted into midfield, with Narris dropping back into defence.

But maybe the most worrying moment for anyone with a blue-and-white-hooped bone in their body came when Madman took a nasty knock. To be fair to Barcelona, there was no question of foul play. It happened when Xavi pumped in a high ball from the right to Albion's far post. Kluivert knew he had no real chance of reaching it. He leapt anyway just to put

Madman off. The keeper caught the ball comfortably. But in trying to avoid charging the Barça striker he twisted away in mid-air, landed on the wrong foot, and fell backwards against the post. Pretty hard.

Craig said afterwards that he heard a crack. Maybe he did, maybe he didn't. But Morty's collision with the woodwork certainly didn't do his back any good. Terry was on for a good three minutes sorting it out. Which, as usual, meant rubbing a cold, wet sponge over it and saying "Run it off, son" (or, as in Madman's case here, "Jump it off"). In the end Madman straightened up and said he was fine. He probably just couldn't take any more sponging.

But the Albion Massive heaved a huge sigh of relief. For there was no substitute goalie on the bench. With CAFC, there rarely was. There *were* other keepers at the club – good ones, too – but they were still learning their trade at the Centre of Excellence, and they didn't yet have the bottle for the big occasion. That was Benny's view, anyway. Besides, Madman was more or less indestructible. "It's all that junk food," was his best mate Chrissie's opinion. "The pies, the pot noodles, the burgers and chips. They give him this cushion of protective flab. Nothing could ever get through that. Not even bullets."

Luckily Madman didn't have to stretch himself much before the ref called a halt to the first ninety minutes. Nor was Hesp called into action too often. A football pitch isn't very long, but sometimes it can take an amazingly long time for something serious to happen in either penalty box. And so the regular part of the game petered out in a mass of midfield scuffling, cagey hit-and-hope punts, and an awful lot of half-crazed noise from van Gaal and Benny Webb.

Webbo kept up the decibel level during the short break before extra-time began. "You can *have* these!" was the gist of everything he said, as far as Luke could make out. There weren't any new orders on tactics or strategy. Which was just as well really. Because if the rest of the lads were feeling as wired-up as Luke, they wouldn't have been able to take them in, let alone obey them.

The fans sounded as drained as the players when they cheered the re-start. It had been a punishing hour and a half. Not much goal-mouth incident, a bit too much gladiator-style combat everywhere else on the pitch. It was a great occasion and everything, but no one could have called it a feast of football.

But on the dogfight went. At least until the deadlock could be broken by a Golden Goal. In point of fact, Rocky and Co would probably have accepted a Silver Goal, or a Bronze one – or even one knocked together out of cardboard and string. *Anything* to get this ultra-tense game won and dusted.

But, as countless millions of fans know only too well, goals don't come to order. And the Golden Goal rule can hold teams back, as well as make them go for it. For who wants to make the mistake that leads to the vital strike? Especially in a major Final being watched all over Europe? In the first period of extra time, caution ruled. Neither side had a worthwhile shot on goal.

Only Luke for Albion and Guardiola for Barça tried anything but the simplest of passes. Luke really had got a second wind. It blew him on into extra time's second phase. As some of the legs around him started looking very weary, he found himself in more and more open spaces. He sprayed around a delightful series of balls but since Albion weren't getting forward in any numbers now, they led to nothing more than a couple of long-range shots from Carl and Dog.

The last few minutes ticked away. Luke just knew what the ITV commentators would be telling all the folks glued to their tellies back at home. "Benny Webb will be preparing his list of penalty-takers." "These are the times when you look to the men in your side with the nerves of steel." "It's never a satisfactory way to decide a major competition – but ooh, it's so *dramatic*!"

Luke wasn't so sure about that. Albion had

already sorted their penalty-taking line-up after Benny's practice session that afternoon. First out of the blocks would be Luke himself, with Cool F taking the second. Against Arsenal in the FA Cup semi-final the previous season, the boys had taken pens four and five – and put them both safely away. "At this level, though," wise old Benny had declared, "the pressure kicks are the first ones. Once you get ahead, the other side's got to catch you up. Luke and Fred can put us in the drivin' seat."

That was an easy thing to say – and to believe – in training. But as the ref blew up for the end of open play, Luke suddenly felt a great new weight on his young shoulders. It was shoot-out time! And he had to draw his gun first!!

25

For the next few minutes almost everyone in the Olympic Stadium found it hard to breathe properly. The tension was unbelievable. As the ref and a gang of UEFA officials sorted out which goal to use, Benny and van Gaal gathered their two sets of players in the centre circle and tried to appear confident about the task ahead. But in Benny's case, he did sound genuinely cocky.

"Lads," he said, resting a hand on Madman's shoulder. "We've come to the moment that this goalkeeper here was born for. Some of you might have wondered just why he *was* born. I'll confess that at times I've asked myself the same question. When he's let mis-hit shots trickle through his legs, when he's flapped at crosses he should never have come for, when he's air-kicked at back passes, I *have* sometimes doubted his destiny in the game. But not now! If there's ever been a better penalty-saver, I've never clapped eyes on him. This is the guy who is going to win us the UEFA Cup!"

"Along with the lads who are gonna stick away their own pens against Hesp," Terry added, smiling at the Famous Five. Already they were standing apart: the guys who had shown up best from the spot that afternoon. Luke and Cool F were always going to be among them. Gaffer too – he had taken all the club's penalties before Luke arrived at Ash Acre. But the last two were slightly surprising. Fourth in line was Carl Davey, and fifth was Casper Franks.

There were no two ways about it. In the practice these two had got better and better with each round of shots. By the end, they were stroking the ball past Gaffer with all the style and grace of Luke and Cool F. But neither of them had ever taken a pen in a real match before. And when Benny announced that they were on his hit-list, even *they* had looked a bit goggle-eyed. Terry too had a quiet word. So did Ruel. But Benny had made his mind up. Carl and Casper would be making their penalty debuts at the sharp end of the UEFA Cup Final.

As the stadium announcer read out the two lists of names, the Albion fans were clearly startled to hear Carl and Casper's names too. They cheered them wildly enough – just like they'd cheered Luke, Frederick and Gaffer. But Luke heard the rumble among them afterwards. And he saw the avalanche of plastic inflatable pineapples raining down on to the pitchside. Craig understood.

With a grin, he trotted over to pick up an armful, then brought them back to the centre circle. The faithful wanted Carl to take a few extra hits before he went up for his spot-kick. Dutifully the wavy-haired wonder bent over, and Craig fired in six perfectly-judged beauties – three on each buttock. That lifted the tension just for a bit, but then it was time for the battle to recommence.

The ref blew his whistle again, the non-marksmen trooped out of the centre-circle, and it was sorted that Barça would go first. That meant Madman waddling down to the goal, waving a clenched fist at the Albion hordes as he did so. He wasn't going to let anybody down tonight. But what a bit of luck that his earlier back injury hadn't been more serious!

The first man up for Barça was Kluivert – looking no less sleek now than he did before two hours of ceaseless running. Luke watched him settle the ball on the spot, turn sharply and stride a short way back. *Miss, miss, miss!* he breathed with all his heart. It wasn't sportsman-like but he just couldn't help it. Nor could any of the other Albion players. Too much was at stake now. Way too much.

Rocky's lot raised an awesome chorus of jeers, boos and catcalls as Kluivert began his run-up. Luke flinched as he made contact. It was a cracker. High and wide to Madman's right. Already a scream of joy went up from the Spanish fans. But it died in their throats as Madman soared spectacularly sideways to swat the ball away past the angle of post and crossbar. For the pot-bellied laddie in green, it was just another day at the office. *He'd saved it!*

Now it was the Albion contingent's turn to raise the roof. But something was wrong. As Luke, Frederick and the rest raced over to congratulate him, Madman didn't spring to his feet to meet them. He stayed rooted to where he had fallen. And one of his hands was clutching at his back again.

Terry rocketed on to the pitch, and got to the keeper before any of the Albion penalty-takers. He'd never moved that fast in his playing days! After a few goes with the sponge Madman staggered to his feet. "Are you OK, son?" Tel kept asking him. "Can you carry on? I mean, it's only four more shots..."

And Madman kept nodding grimly back, wincing at times, but still nodding. Luke was worried by that, but he had an even more pressing matter to think about. Hesp was already in place between the sticks. The ball was back on the spot. It was now Green Junior's job to do his level best to rifle it into the net.

He tried to block out all the sound – from

friend and foe alike – as he re-settled the ball on the spot. (You always have to do that. It's like when you cross a road at traffic lights. You always have to press the button yourself, even if five people in front of you have already done it.) As he stepped back again, he didn't think about missing, he didn't think of scoring. He just stared, hard, at the right-hand corner of the goal, skipped in, then blasted it towards the *left*.

Hesp hadn't been fooled. He dived the correct way. But Luke's shot was too fast, too low, too accurate. He was beaten all ends up. Even before the ball nestled against the stanchion, Luke turned away to salute his score. He'd done it! Albion had their noses in front – just as Benny had wanted them to!

After giving Luke a huge hug, Madman made his way back over to the goal – this time to face Frank de Boer. There was no way now that he could hide his pain. Every slow step was agony for the guy. He really had done something naughty to his back. But Madman's heart was as big as his stomach. And that was something de Boer hadn't reckoned on.

Luke guessed the Dutch star's intention as he ran in. He thought that if he aimed it just where Kluivert had put it, Madman wouldn't fancy repeating the save that had hurt him so badly. He gave the ball an almighty wallop. And it arrowed in even closer to the angle of post and crossbar than Kluivert's kick. But once again Madman rose to the occasion – not just stopping the thunderbolt but *catching* it! And maybe that was one touch of heroics too far.

Still clutching the ball, he plummeted to the ground like two sacks of potatoes. He should have kept his hands free, to try to break his fall. And from the roar he gave on impact (of pure pain, not triumph) Luke knew that he would be taking no further part in this shoot-out. Again Terry rushed on. But this time Morty needed more than a magic sponge. Half a dozen of the players came on too, and although Madman protested all the way, they carted him off the pitch. They had to. He couldn't even stand unassisted, let alone walk. What he needed, and eventually got, was a full course of treatment from a chiropractor.

But that was all in the future. Here and now Albion had a problem. A pretty tricky problem, when you thought about it. For here they were, well ahead in the penalty stakes, but suddenly minus a goalkeeper. That's quite a major minus when everything depends on you stopping the other lot from scoring.

For a few mad minutes, it looked very bleak indeed. Out in the centre-circle there was a huge ruck as both sets of players and officials argued with UEFA's head honchos over what should happen next. Barça didn't seem to want

Albion to *have* a keeper to face their remaining three kicks.

In the end, however, common sense won out. Gaffer – Madman's usual emergency stand-in – was allowed to don the goalie's green jersey. But as Luke watched him tug it over his head, he knew that every Albion fan and player was thinking the same chilling thing: *He'll do his best, but he's not Madman...* Morty was a marvel in these showdowns, Gaffer was just mortal. It was like having Clark Kent standing in at the shortest notice for Superman.

But he didn't have to put himself on the line just yet. First Albion had a kick of their own, their second, so up stepped Cool F. He was absolutely the best possible person to take some heat out of this situation. Hesp did his best to put him off by jerking about and bobbing up and down. But F is for Focus as well as for Frederick. And F for Failure never *ever* crossed his mind.

Hesp dived right, Frederick shot left. There was no getting away from this: after two pens apiece, Albion were two goals to nil in the lead!!! And Rocky and Co let the whole of Rome know just what they thought about that!

Meanwhile, after high-fiving Frederick, Gaffer started the lonely trek over to the goal. It was so weird to see him in Madman's green jersey. It must have felt pretty weird to him too, thought Luke – especially when he turned and got an eyeful of the player he would have to face. Rivaldo!!!

The brilliant Brazilian didn't quite grin as he set the ball on the spot. But he didn't look too nervous either. Everyone in the stadium knew what a missile-launcher his left foot was. Him against Madman really would have been the utlimate head-to-head. Instead, now he had to stick it past Gaffer. But, thanks to Benny, Manno had at least had a bit of practice in goal that afternoon.

"You'll Never Beat The Gaffer!"

roared Rocky's mob as Rivaldo stole in. And it was true enough – no one had ever beaten him from the spot before. But then again, this was the first real penalty he'd ever been asked to save. And he nearly did it too. With phenomenal power Rivaldo hit it straight down the middle. Gaffer stood his ground and got his left hand to it. But that just sent it higher into the net behind him – and Barça had pulled the score back to 1-2!

With the Spanish fans going bananas, Gaffer strode back shaking his head – and shaking his hand as well. The hand that had got in the way of Rivaldo's piledriver. "What's up?" asked Carl. "You haven't done *your*self in now too?"

"Nah, I'll be OK," said Gaffer, still shaking it. "Just tingles a bit, that's all."

"Well, forget about that now," Casper told his captain. "You're taking the next pen, remember?"

From the look Gaffer gave him, he really might have forgotten. In all the excitement, it was hard to keep track of who was meant to be doing what and when. So around turned the skipper, hoping to do a Rivaldo now on Hesp. But Luke could see that his hand was giving him real grief. He kept on flexing his fingers as he ran in... Then he clenched them in a fist of utter despair as his shot cannoned against Hesp's right-hand post and came straight back to him.

He'd missed! Both sides had taken three kicks, Albion were 2-1 ahead. This was getting a bit too close for comfort now.

As Gaffer took the short walk from the spot to the goal, Guardiola couldn't get forward quick enough to take his potshot. Luke and Fred exchanged blank looks. A keeper had to be mentally "right" to face a pen. But how could he be anywhere near right when he'd just missed one himself?

Gaffer winced as he pulled on Madman's gloves. Guardiola saw that. He was *well* up for this, Luke could tell. He didn't so much walk back after settling the ball – he strutted. Then in he charged.

Keepers aren't meant to move until the ball is struck. Almost all of them do, though. But this time Gaffer didn't budge till after Guardiola let fly. To be frank, he didn't even see it coming. Or rather – *going*. For the ball rocketed upwards so sharply that it sailed a good five yards over the crossbar – and was still rising when it was swallowed up by the crowd! He'd missed by a mile!!

"You'll Never Beat The Gaffer!"

rang out around the stadium from thousands of English fans keen to give all the credit to the non-moving netminder. The players too rushed to mob their skipper like a hero, but sternly he held up his gloves to keep them away. *He* knew the score here.

"It's in our hands now," he said. "If we score one more time, we've won this thing." He grabbed Carl's shoulder. "It's up to you, son. Do it for us."

Carl cocked his head. "I'm up for it, Gaffer," he gulped. "Make no mistake about that. But haven't we got *two* more kicks? I mean, I'm only the fourth in line – and then there's Casper to go next."

The others rolled their eyes. "We're 2-1 up, right?" Luke tried to explain. "If you score now, that will make it 3-1 to us. So even if Barça *scored* with their last kick, it would only pull them back to 3-2. We would already have won!"

Carl nodded, still not certain. "But how about Casper's kick?"

"Look," yelled Gaffer, grabbing his shoulder again and starting to frogmarch him towards the penalty spot. "It's really dead simple. You score – we win."

"Oh – right," Luke heard Carl say before his voice was swallowed up by the crowd's chaotic din. But then even the fans' jeers and cheers stopped registering in the Studless Sensation's ears. As he watched Carl go forward, all he heard was a ghostly roll-call of the European sides that Albion had beaten to get this far: Sliema Wanderers of Malta, Fenerbahce of Turkey, Bayern Munich of Germany, Spartak Moscow of Russia, Paris St Germain of France…

All that fabulous football, all those goals and thrills and frights and journeys. And now it had come down to this: a single kick from a single player. A player who needed fruit flung at him before he felt confident of scoring. A player who was still doing mental arithmetic – wrongly – as he bent to place the ball.

If Luke was absolutely honest, Carl wouldn't have been *his* choice as kicker number four. In his time he'd scored some cracking goals in open play. And he really was a great lad and everything. But to take such a mega-pressure kick as this? Whew – close call! But that was what Benny Webb in his wisdom had decreed. And Benny Webb's wisdom was what everyone had gone on strike for. So this, now, was going to be the big moment of truth.

Luke crossed his fingers, his feet, most of the

hairs on his head and what felt like all of his intestines. Every Albion lover in the world was throwing an invisible pineapple, hard, at Carl's bottom.

Deadly Mr Davey took a mere two steps back, paused, then surged forward. He didn't smash his shot. He didn't go for power at all. But he didn't go for placement either. Not for him the shot that edges just inside the post before nestling against the back stanchion. So if he didn't hit it hard, and he didn't aim for the corner, he must have made an absolute horlicks of his shot – right?

Wrong! A hundred times wrong! Make that a *million* times! Because with a calmness that would have made Laid-back Des Lynam look like a gibbering wreck, he *chipped* his first proper penalty into the centre of the net as Hesp spread himself wide to his left. The ball dinked up in a lovely little arc over the keeper's flailing legs. And Carl had put so much backspin on it that it stopped, dead, exactly where it landed – three feet over the line. *It was there!*

Had Benny been right to give the fourth kick to Carl? You bet your bottom lira! As the Albion faithful went volcanic Carl turned away, looking only moderately chuffed. Clearly he had forgotten that he hadn't simply scored – he had won the flipping Cup as well! But he had the rest of his life to get to grips with the maths of it. In the meantime he had the entire staff of Castle Albion FC – including an hysterical Mrs Bowman – burying him alive in a human pyramid!

"*You did it! You did it! You did it!*" bellowed Benny to no one in particular from the middle of the pile of limbs. Then Luke felt a huge sloppy kiss on his head – but Dennis had him in a headlock so he couldn't turn to see who had planted it. Nor could he see who was ripping off his trainers – although later his headmistress told him that it was her! She hurled them where the Albion fans were thickest – or where they'd *been* thickest. For, like the head, thousands on thousands of them were now on the pitch, turning the pyramid into a mountain.

"I love you, Carl!" roared a voice that could only have been Rocky's. ("And I do too, Mr Wavy-Haired Davey!" squealed little Polly.) "Oh, Luke, Luke, Luke!" screamed a familiar weepy voice, as someone else tugged bodies out of the way to get to him. It was Rod doing the weeping and screaming; Luke's mum digging her way in towards him. In the end they both got there, hauled Luke up then knocked him straight back over with the force of their double embrace.

"That's the most fun I've ever had without my gardening gloves on!" roared Luke's mum. "Though why on earth you started taking free kicks when you could have carried on playing proper football, I'll never know. So does this mean you'll be in the Premier League next season?"

"No, but who cares about the Premier League!" cried another unmistakable voice. And an equally unmistakable vice-like grip on his shoulders told Luke that his grandpa was behind him. "*We've won the UEFA Cup, laddie!*"

"Ooh Luke," wept his nan, dancing a jig in front of him with Ruel Bibbo, "I never... A grandson of mine... Oh, it's really all too much!"

Then Luke caught a whiff of incense – and there was TAFKAG, waving an inflatable blue-and-white-hooped guitar. He had to be the least likely-looking club chairman in world football, but what a start he'd made to his boardroom career! "Oh, baby!" he grinned, proudly hugging his son. "Groovy gig or what? Hey, I can feel a song coming on: *Cheesecloth Chairman's Party Rag...*"

But before he could start thrashing at his plastic guitar, Terry and Rocky hoisted him up and whisked him off to where countless fans went down on their knees to him, wailing "*We Are Not Worthy! We Are Not Worthy!*"

As the on-pitch mayhem got worse, worried-looking UEFA officials darted about, trying to round up all the Albion players to make the presentations. By the time they'd succeeded, most of the Barça players had already received their runners-up medals over by the touchline. The Albion lads went to shake hands with them. They looked so stunned. It really was no way to lose a final.

Then up went the Albion players. As each one turned away to hold up his medal, Benny Webb's Blue-and-white Army pierced the night sky with their unbelievable din. And at last Gaffer went forward, to collect not just his medal but the fabulous trophy too, with its blue and white ribbons. When he thrust it above his head, the Albion Massive stretched their lungs to bursting-point with:

"We've Won, And You Know We Have!
We've WON, And You Know We Have!"

And they had. They really, really had! That night Benny Webb's Albion had passed into the European Hall of Fame. No one would ever be able to take this away from them. Luke felt so puffed up with pride, he thought he might start floating. Cool F, standing next to him now, just kept nodding down at his medal. And when at last he looked up and his eyes met Luke's, they grinned.

Both of them were so clearly thinking the same thing: that dreams *do* come true, and that – quite frankly – it doesn't get much better than this. They each reached into their socks, took out a few blades of hallowed Ash Acre grass, kissed them, and let them flutter down on to the Olympic turf. They'd *done* it!

Then ITV's Gary Newbon was in front of them with his roving mike. "Lads, lads!" he yelled. "Fantastic! Incredible! Magnificent! So what's next?"

"You know what?" Luke said dreamily above the racket all round. "Just this once, I'm going to leave my geography homework till tomorrow night."

"Rockin'," agreed Cool F, as Benny flashed by in a sheepskin blur on the shoulders of fifty jubilant fans. "And we've got TAFKAG's gig to take in."

"Sorry, Frederick," barked Gary, adjusting his earpiece. "I didn't quite catch that last bit. Where did you lads say you were on your way to?"

Albion's schoolboy superstars smiled at each other. Then they ducked closer in to the microphone. After such a triumph, such a night, such a Cup run, what could they say? "*We're not on our way to anywhere!*" they cried. "*We've arrived! In FOOTBALL HEAVEN!*"